MW01633865

FATHERLAND

BOOKS BY VICTORIA SHORR

Mid-Air

The Plum Trees

Midnight

Backlands

FATHERLAND

A Novel

VICTORIA SHORR

W. W. NORTON & COMPANY

Independent Publishers Since 1923

This is a work of fiction. Names, characters, places, and incidents are the product of the author's imagination or are used fictitiously. Any resemblance to actual events, locales, or persons, living or dead, is entirely coincidental.

Copyright © 2026 by Victoria Shorr

All rights reserved
Printed in the United States of America
First Edition

For information about permission to reproduce selections from this book, write to Permissions, W. W. Norton & Company, Inc., 500 Fifth Avenue, New York, NY 10110

For information about special discounts for bulk purchases, please contact W. W. Norton Special Sales at specialsales@wwnorton.com or 800-233-4830

Manufacturing by Versa Press
Book design by Daniel Lagin
Production manager: Daniel Van Ostenbridge

ISBN: 978-1-324-11755-1

W. W. Norton & Company, Inc.
500 Fifth Avenue, New York, NY 10110
www.wwnorton.com

W. W. Norton & Company Ltd.
15 Carlisle Street, London W1D 3BS

Authorized EU representative:
EAS, Mustamäe tee 50, 10621 Tallinn, Estonia

1 2 3 4 5 6 7 8 9 0

To B.W.

In Memoriam. Infinite Thanks.

What was the rock my gliding childhood struck,
And what bright unreal path has led me here?

PHILIP LARKIN

— I —

A WEDDING PARTY

It was almost surreal, he thought, looking out over the whole group, all of them smiling, happy, none of them knowing. He'd even been part of the wedding party, one of the ushers for his brother-in-law, who wouldn't, he figured, be speaking to him in the morning. He'd smiled for the photographers, posed with his wife, posed with her family, for the last time.

Unless he didn't go.

That possibility had crossed his mind, as he watched Josie walk down the aisle with her little basket of flowers. She looked particularly sweet and touching, so serious, her sweet face almost angelic, and he'd wanted to pick her up and hug her, and his wife too, a bridesmaid, looking pretty again for the first time since the baby. Her hair had gotten longer finally, and she'd lost the weight, and it had occurred to him that he could still stay put. Make a call and come up with something, anything, some good reason he wouldn't be there tonight.

But he wasn't making that call. He was going. First of all, because he wanted to go. Had a need to go, a taste in his mouth for that pale skin, that tall, cool remoteness—former remoteness, but there were still traces. He could still call it back.

He glanced at his watch—she would already be there, waiting. Had already taken a shower, just as he liked, and put on the cotton nightgown. Or not, it didn't matter. He would throw her in himself, if it came to it. Like the last time, when they didn't get out of bed for half a day.

He looked up—into his mother's eyes. Worried eyes—about what, though? Did she know? Sense something? No one knew, but why did she have that look? Why was she watching him? Why was she even here?

Still, it had been nice of the family to ask his parents, to always ask them, though they never really fit. His father, in his cheap striped suit, his mother in that dress with the faded silk flower pinned to the shoulder. Lora had wanted him to give her a nice pearl pin for Christmas, and he should have, he would. Next year.

Not that she'd need it then, because this would be the end of these invitations. Too bad for his mother, but he'd already done plenty for her. Made her proud, first in high school, where he was everyone's friend and was voted most popular boy in the class, though the others had more of everything else. Cars, spending cash—their fathers made money, were shopkeepers, lawyers, druggists. His father drove a cab, but despite that, he was the one with "all the charm," as the yearbook had put it. And then college and the Navy in the War, and med school. All good, and then his marriage, the three children, the house—for his parents, now that he thought about it. For all of them, and what about him?

They were lining up for another photograph. The whole family, together, smiling. Him too. *Ha, ha,* a little voice inside was saying.

Wait for me, he was whispering, to the other side of town.

Shortly after that, he went to his wife with a worried look. He'd just called in to the Medical Dental Bureau— the sick child he was treating had been taken to the hospital. They'd been calling him, he told her. He'd swing by now, to check, and be home later, if everything was okay. Meanwhile, his father would drive her and Josie home in his cab.

Years later, Josie came upon the photograph of that night, from her uncle's wedding. The family were seated at a table, her grandparents smiling, her mother beautiful, despite the bridesmaid dress. She herself was standing behind, next to her father, but blocked from view by someone. Only the side of her head was visible, one ponytail and a ribbon, and her shoulder, but you could see his arm around her. For the last time maybe, she thought, looking at the picture, caught, fatefully, on camera. The last hug from him that she would have taken naturally, for granted, without desperation, without hunger or thirst.

HOWARD AND ELECTRA

"You didn't tell her."

Howard could tell from the sound of her steps, trudging up the back stairs. Her face confirmed it.

"I couldn't. She was down there with the baby, happy and all—"

Electra lay down on the bed. It was April, but already stuffy up here on the third floor. "She loves that man."

Howard nodded. Sad to see up close, the way she looked at him when he was home, which wasn't often these days. Sad too the way she still believed. But he, Howard, no longer believed. The man was moving out, little by little, like a sneak. He had Howard carrying out his suits, one by one, every time he came home, as if he needed them at the hospital, and some of the shoes, spacing the others so it looked like he still lived here, in this house that he'd taken so much trouble to put together just the way he wanted it, not even a year ago.

And then he'd hired them, Howard and Electra, to run it that way. Serve him breakfast on a silver tray in the dining room, away from the children, and keep the carnations he liked to pin in his buttonhole in a vase in the hallway. Freeze peaches for him in the summer, so come January he'd have them for his cornflakes.

And they did it just right, kept it all humming for him, and she did too, even put on a smile, nights when he came home, though other nights they heard her crying. And she smiled too through the parties he liked to throw, though she still looked exhausted, the baby was only a few months old then. But he'd liked showing off his house, his life, bringing in Alonzo Wilson, the policeman, to tend bar in a white coat, like he must have seen in some old movie, because it wasn't as if he'd been born to any of this.

She had, or closer, anyway, and was nice, easy to work for. Only time she got nervous was when he did—his steak was underdone, the shirt he wanted was still in the laundry basket. Then he'd criticize not them but her. Electra told Howard that she'd overheard him complaining because he'd had to drive her old Chevy the other day, when his fancy new Buick was in the shop.

He'd come in, thrown down the keys, and said to Lora, "Your car drives like a truck!" As if it were her fault.

And she'd smiled and half apologized, said something like, "Oh, it's not so bad, I like the old thing."

Electra shook her head. "I'd have had a different answer for him!"

"I know it," said Howard, and they laughed. "The good doctor," they called him, with increasing irony.

"Because what kind of a man drives better than his wife?" asked Electra.

On the other hand, he was the one who paid them—more than the going rate for a couple, but that wouldn't last, if he really was moving out. There was no way she'd need a butler to carry her frozen peaches to the dining room. She didn't even eat them, didn't even give them to the children. Saved them all for him.

Alonzo Wilson was the one who'd told him that he had another woman, "not for the first time," but this one was said to be "in the family way."

"Rumor has it," said Alonzo Wilson.

Howard's heart had sunk when he heard it. They'd known that there were girlfriends—wasn't Electra the one washing their lipstick off his collars, like in a bad song? Different colors too, cheap pink, cherry-red—"How many women does that man have?" she'd fume to Howard. But a pregnant one was another story.

And the worst part was that his wife still didn't know—"Out cold in the Seven Sleepers den," was how Electra put it. Lora was still smiling brightly when he came home, rushing the children away from him—"Daddy is tired, he works so hard!"—and then making sure Howard fixed his drink just right, and Electra carried his steaks and casseroles to the table, where she'd sit with her smile, and her hair nicely brushed and a new dress on, one she'd dieted and exercised to fit into, all those sit-ups and stretches on the floor. And then, just as she was telling him about the children, the cute things they'd done and said, he'd get a call, and, finishing his supper, explain that he had to go back to the hospital.

But Electra was the one who answered the phone, and "it wasn't any hospital calling," she would say, shrugging, to Howard.

Which was why she'd got Howard to apply for the job at the community center, as soon as she heard they needed both a man and a cook with good references. "That's you and me," she told him. "The good doctor" would give them the reference. He never said no to anyone, except his wife and kids.

And they'd got the job, but hadn't been able to face giving her notice, and now there was no more time. They felt bad about that, bad about everything, nothing good about it—and when Electra went downstairs to tell her just then, she'd found her on the floor, doing her stretches, and lost heart.

The baby was nearby, playing with some toy horses. He had just started crawling. Eight months. Very cute. Never cried.

Electra made an excuse—asked if she wanted some coffee or anything—and then went upstairs and told Howard he had to do it. It was Wednesday. They were leaving this weekend. He took a breath and went downstairs.

"Sorry to bother you," Howard started, and she looked up, knowing something—sensing that something was up, and just nodded when he told her about the job at the community center. He had some excuses, but didn't need them. She told him right off that she could see it was a step up.

"Does Dr. Brier know?" she asked. Worried, first and foremost, about his drink, his peaches.

"Uh, I'm—uh, not sure," he lied. He didn't tell her that it was good Dr. Brier who had given them their reference.

"Problem is, we have to leave on Friday."

"This Friday? Couldn't you stay one more week? Till I find someone?"

"The job starts Monday. I'm sorry—"

And that was true, both parts of it. But it wasn't as if he had any choices here. There weren't many jobs in 1956 for Black men in this town. The steel unions were closed to them. The railroads were shedding conductors and porters. True, you could find work at the wrecking yards and garages, hard work at low pay, where you'd come home covered with grease and dirt, but Howard had moved on from that. This wasn't his first job as a butler. He'd done some bartending too.

But for him to work at a community center meant he was no longer a personal servant. He'd probably have more hands-on work than here, since Lora had an old handyman she called in when something needed to be fixed—Simeon Richardson, a minister in one of the Baptist churches. The little girl, Josie, had seen the cross on the old man's car, and asked Howard what "clergy" meant. He explained, and saw the child processing the fact that a Black man who was a minister of the church could still be up a ladder in old blue overalls at her house. Already knowing at age six—or was she seven?—that any of the white "clergy" she knew would never be up anyone's ladder, except possibly their own.

And even that was unlikely, with good men like Sim Richardson to show up and do it for them, so as to get through his week and pay his light bill. And then go down on Sunday, in his own suit, to a church that could barely pay him, which meant he and the rest of the Black clergy in town did it for love. Which was probably the difference, why when you sat and listened to them, it rang true, you found yourself feeling something, but when those well-paid white ones started preaching, best anyone could do was stay awake to sneak a peek at their watches. He knew. He'd been a janitor at a couple of white churches.

Well, he'd miss Sim at his next job—he'd probably be the one up the ladder there, at least at first. Ordered around, subjected, depending on who was calling the shots, but he knew too how not to dwell on it. To dwell instead on how he'd slowly make it work out for him and Electra. Work his own way into trust, and then indispensability. Into organizing the center's dinners, their bingo, their family nights, with Electra, indispensable too, in the kitchen. Maybe even move up to helping in the office with billing and purchase orders, if they'd let him. He could do it. He'd done well at school, taken the business classes, and the math.

This was his chance, maybe—possibly. But even if it wasn't, if he couldn't work his way up to a spot of dignity, at least he could earn enough there, and steadily, so he and Electra could buy a small house on the South Side. One bedroom would do it, since there weren't any children.

Just as well.

"I'm sorry," he said to the woman, Mrs. Brier. Lora.

"I understand," she said. "I'll have your wages on Friday."

Would she? he wondered. Only if her husband came back between now and then. If not, maybe he'd go by the hospital, or around to his office. He'd get him to pay, one way or the other. He owed them two weeks.

Lora got up from the chair and picked up the baby. "We're going for a walk."

"You want me to call Electra to take him?"

"No, thanks, I'd like a walk myself." She managed a smile and put the baby in the buggy and wheeled him down the drive. Howard picked up the toys, looked around the room. A nice place, with the bookshelves, and then the bar, in the back, with a sink and running water. "A wet bar," Alonzo Wilson called it. Said it made his job a lot easier. Most folks just had one of those carts on wheels. You had to go back and forth from the kitchen to wash the glasses.

Well, Alonzo Wilson wouldn't be back here anytime soon. Until she got herself married again.

But that wasn't even in the cards, said Electra. She was still in love with her no-good husband. Still telling herself that he'd be back.

How could he not? she, Lora, was wondering right then, as she pushed the buggy down the sidewalk. Toward the park—she didn't want to go by the school and pick up Josie, she needed a breath, needed not to have to talk. Needed to figure out how to run the house for him without Howard and Electra. She could cook, enough anyway, and she could get her mother to make some things, and she could mix him a drink, although she couldn't sit with him and have the children out of the way. She needed help for that.

Or not—that was the irony, she guessed. She knew why Howard was leaving, or why Howard thought he was leaving, but there was no way her husband could walk out on her, on them. His three children, whom he loved, surely, even if he didn't love her? He had to love them—what man didn't love his children? And theirs were beautiful, they were good and smart and fun and lovely. All good, and the baby wasn't even a year old and never cried, smiled all the time. Even at him, when he hadn't been home for a week, with the worst excuses in the history of the world. They needed him "at the hospital." One "emergency" and then another, although he wasn't that kind of a doctor. He was a general practitioner, the kind you went to in the morning with the flu.

But she was all right with it, with any of it, as long as he didn't move out. As long as it didn't become official. As long as there was hope, the chance of him coming through this, whatever it was, especially for the children. She'd watched their daughter the other morning, snuggling up in bed with him, her head on his chest. A smile on the child's face that was never there when he wasn't home.

But then he'd shrugged her off with impatience, told her not to breathe in his face. The girl was only seven years old, but she'd seen her take it in. Seen it bewilder her, and Lora had a moment of wondering then if it might not be better if he did leave. Before much more of that.

But no, it wouldn't be better, it was inconceivable. No one got divorced. They figured it out, and she would too. They would. She'd go to him next time he came home, ask him what she could do, she would do anything. Even accept whatever it was—yes, another woman—because she knew it wouldn't last. It was her he loved, her and the children, and beyond that, his life. His house on a tree-lined boulevard, on the principal street in town. He'd grown up on backstreets, but now that was over. He'd brought in Molly Waldhorn, the top decorator, to put it together the way he wanted it, and had hosted parties to show the world.

And the world had congratulated him, clapped him on the back and told him that he'd married well, he had a lovely wife, beautiful children. Surely that was something to him. To her it was everything, their life together. He couldn't just kick it all to pieces.

He wouldn't. She took a breath. It was a beautiful day. Spring. The baby had fallen asleep in the buggy. She turned for home.

The children saw Howard and Electra carrying their things down the back steps.

"Are you leaving?"

"Just for a little bit," said Electra. She fixed the girl's ponytail. She needed a haircut. Her mother must not have noticed.

Josie was a pretty child, would probably have a good life, all in all. Electra would sometimes sing her "Summertime," when she put her to bed, and it had seemed true, there, in that nice bedroom. Her daddy was rich, and her ma was good-looking. *"Don't you cry,"* Electra had sung, and meant it. Nothing to cry about.

She hadn't figured, though, on him going bad like this. The men in this town stayed married. All his friends—the lawyers, the doctors, the CPAs—these men picked a wife, had the kids, and called it good, called it their life, and they were happy, who wouldn't be? They bought nice, safe houses, on the North Side, and he'd bought the nicest of all, and should have been happiest.

Too bad for his wife—she could have, should have, married one of the others. She was prettier than her friends, could have had her pick. Had had her pick, Irene Davis told Electra the other day, when they were shaking their heads over it. Irene had just started working for her mother then, and had seen the whole thing unroll. Said that Lora was in her last year in high school, and all set to go to college in Indiana, and her father had already paid the fee, when he—her future husband—came home from the Navy in his white uniform, fixed his eye on her, and got her to run away with him and get married. Her parents were shocked, everyone was. Everyone had liked him. He was her older brother's best friend. They'd all thought he was hanging around the house for him.

But it was the war then, Irene said to Electra, things were crazy in those years. Messed up her own life too. Not college, in her case—she hadn't even finished high school, but she'd had a decent job ironing at a laundry in Sandusky, and had moved up to running the mangle, doing the sheets instead of shirts with the same pay. But when the war broke out, "We heard what they were paying up at the Willys factory, over in Toledo, so we moved over there."

But it turned out they weren't hiring Black people, men or women, so it hadn't worked out.

She hadn't mentioned a husband before, and Electra didn't ask. She could imagine the parts Irene didn't put in. From the hopes and dreams of the Willys factory in Toledo to the back door of this house a hundred and fifty miles away—she'd trodden the same path herself, just a generation later. She too had dropped out of high school when the next war came, Korea, looking for a job in Cleveland and had ended up at the same back door as Irene, climbing the same back steps.

But at least she'd learned to cook along the way. An old Gullah woman from the South had taught her, little by little, more so she could help her out, do her job too. That was a big, fancy house with three women working there, and a man in the garden, and they all had to eat, not just the owners and their children. Steak and lamb chops for the dining room, with sauces made with lemons they got sent every week from a grocer in Pittsburgh, and the cook set her, Electra, to work on the boiled meat for them in the kitchen, which they all said was better anyway. More taste to it.

That cook gave her her start, but she was old and mean, wouldn't let the children in her kitchen, as she called it. She knew some spells from down South, and once put a curse on all the girls working there, that none of them would marry.

So they'd gone crying to the woman of the house, and she brought in her priest, a Roman Catholic, even though they were Baptist, all of them. But he'd come in a purple gown, with silver and smoke, and chanted, and they'd all knelt down, let the smoke waft over them, and felt better afterward. And sure enough, soon after that she'd met Howard, in uniform too, only it was Army, not Navy, so khaki, not white, but she'd been the one in white when they got married.

She was nineteen then—she'd almost forgotten that whole incident, with the cook and her voodoo. Although it had come back to her soon after they'd started work for the doctor in his new house. Right when they were moving in—she and Howard had been carrying some outdoor furniture around, to the back patio, and Josie had called out to them, "Bunnies!"

She'd gone over to look, and there, in the well of one of the basement windows, were three newborn rabbits, curled close together in a nest, but white and dead. The mother must have abandoned them—the house had been vacant for a few months, and the activity of the move, the men, the trucks, had probably sent her fleeing. Leaving the three to die here—too bad it was three.

Josie noticed too. "Like Willie, Timmy, and me," she said.

Electra picked her up and carried her away. She had half a thought to ask Lora to bring in a priest, in purple, but wasn't sure if such a thing even existed thereabouts. How you would even start to find one.

So, "Nah, they're just rabbits," she said to Josie, and called Howard to get rid of them. But no one would have called it a good sign.

"Are you going far?" Josie was asking her now. The child looked stricken.

"No, just nearby," she told her, "and Howard and Electra will come back soon to see you," though they didn't. Josie sometimes saw Howard from afar, at the community center where they worked for years, and sometimes he'd come and say hello, but it made her uneasy, though she couldn't say why. He'd always been so nice, but he called back something she didn't like to remember, and as for Electra, she never laid eyes on her again.

MARGARET CAULEY

That night, Lora took the children to her mother's for supper. He hadn't come home for a few days, and though she didn't want to miss him in case he did come—was desperate not to miss him—she was even more desperate to find someone to help her, also in case he came, so there could be a nice dinner for him. Someone at least to get the children out of his way, so he could sit and relax a bit. So she could comb her hair and mix his drink for him.

It wouldn't be like Howard, in his nice white coat, bespeaking all right with the world, but a nice woman would be fine now, anyway all she could handle. Especially since she wasn't sure not only how she could pay a maid, but how to buy food next week. There was no money left in her account, and her husband wasn't answering her calls.

She half considered leaving a message with the Medical Dental Bureau: *Will Dr. Brier please call his wife and children? Or at least drop off some cash?*

She pulled up to her parents' house, with the three of them in the car, the baby in a little carrying case in the back with Josie holding on to him, Willie standing on the seat beside her, jumping around, then crying when she held out her arm to restrain him, but it was only a few blocks, thank goodness.

Irene opened the door for them. The children ran into her thin arms. She slipped Willie one of her gumdrops to stop him from crying, and took them all into the kitchen. Lora's father, home from work, was in the living room, reading his paper, though they'd recently gotten a TV set and were about to watch Huntley-Brinkley, which came on at six p.m. Then dinner. Lora hadn't told her mother that they were coming, but her mother was famous for being able to accommodate ten extra dinner guests on any given night. Although of course the children wouldn't eat much, or Lora either.

Her mother noticed. "You're looking thin," she said during dinner, "have some more," to which Lora said something about the weight she'd gained with the baby. Which her husband had already started mentioning right after the baby was born—though she didn't tell her mother that.

It had been a tough pregnancy, following close upon

another one, a baby she'd lost, and she'd felt sick and scared all the way through. There was a new drug her obstetrician had mentioned, for morning sickness—thalidomide, not yet on the U. S. market. He didn't have access yet, but thought maybe her husband could get ahold of some for her, if he made a few calls. And she wrote down the name and asked him, but he kept forgetting, and the months had rolled on, culminating in an emergency C-section with some complications, from which she still didn't feel completely recovered, and a wonderful baby whose father had barely spoken his name.

She was contemplating during dinner how to ask her parents for some money. Thinking that it might be better to slip upstairs into her mother's room and swipe a twenty from her wallet, or even a fiver. The problem was that there was help in the house, and someone else might be blamed. Not Irene or Sim, but there was a cleaning woman who sometimes came.

Because it wasn't as if her mother wouldn't notice. Twenty dollars she would definitely notice. Maybe even figure out who had really taken it, which would be almost as damning as asking, when her husband did come back. If her mother figured out that her daughter's larceny meant that he had left her with no money.

Still, there was very little left in the house. She'd gone through the car ashtray for change, and all her pockets, her raincoat, where she'd been overjoyed to find three dollar bills. Then she'd gone into his closet and searched through the pockets of his clothes and found a few quarters that he always kept on hand for tips. Great, except that it was then that she realized most of his suits were gone. She had stood there, trying to figure, to think. Had he taken them to the cleaner? But the cleaner came and picked up at the house. And he wouldn't have given them to the man without her noticing, or had he? One time? If he'd been home once, when Creed the Cleaner rang the bell?

But some of his pants and shirts were still hanging there, and most of his shoes. So it had to be okay, he still lived there, clearly, though by that night at her parents he'd been absent for long enough for her not to know what to do about money. Short-term.

She could just ask her parents, but then they would know and hold it against him, not forgive him, and it would be awkward, once he was back—

"You're not eating," her mother said to her. It was stuffed peppers, something her father liked, one of his Hungarian dishes.

"If I'd known you were coming," said her mother, "we could have had something for the children," but the children had been happy enough to retreat into the kitchen with

Irene, so she could fry up some of last night's chicken for them, and tell them again about "little Bobby Greenleaf."

Josie was fascinated by the tale, though Irene was the only one who would ever talk to her about it. The "sweetest little boy there ever was," according to Irene, and just her age, when he was kidnapped and brutally killed, not too far from there.

"On this street?"

No, but like this street, only over in Missouri, out West, almost. Josie tried to picture it, from the cowboy shows she loved, but those shows didn't have schools, and this had happened in a school, like hers. A woman had come to little Bobby Greenleaf's school and told a teacher—like hers—that she was his aunt, and that his mother had had a heart attack and sent her to fetch him home.

And he hadn't said a word, hadn't denied it, which had Irene shaking her head, but Josie understood. She knew how scary grown-ups could be, especially strangers, at school, where there were lots of grown-ups you didn't know. And she knew why Bobby Greenleaf hadn't dared say a word, but just gave his hand to this woman he'd never seen before, "as good as gold," said Irene Davis, and the woman had taken him out of school that day and killed him.

In cold blood, said Irene—whatever that meant. Right

outside her own house, and she'd dug a hole in the flower garden, and by the time the nun who ran the school called his house to make inquiries, and then the truth came out, and all the police in the whole state went looking, little Bobby Greenleaf was already dead and buried in his grave—

Josie's grandmother came in. "Whose grave?"

"Little Bobby Greenleaf's!" cried Josie.

"Bobby Greenlease? The kidnapping? But you'll frighten them, Irene!" and that was the end of that, at least until Josie got Irene alone again. Because there was a lot here still that she had to know. She could see little Bobby Greenleaf, looking just like Charles Stanley in her kindergarten class. Also a good little boy with pale blue eyes and blond hair who always kept quiet and didn't run around outside with the rest of them, and would have given his hand, like little Bobby Greenleaf, to any woman who came to their school to get him too.

Josie knew just what she looked like too, that woman, with tight gray curls and an ugly wool coat like Aunt Ethel's, but what she couldn't see was Bobby Greenleaf's grave. Irene said there were flowers, but couldn't there be tiny green leaves too? They'd once been given little green leaves to paste onto a tree in art, and it was beautiful. Was that like little Bobby Greenleaf's grave?

She wanted to ask Irene, but Irene was in the living room, telling her mother and grandmother about her sister, Margaret, who needed a job. She was a good cook, said Irene, and honest, reliable. Her grandmother said she sounded perfect, and Lora agreed. She didn't mention the little fact that she didn't have the money to pay her right then, so it was settled that Margaret would start right away, as soon as she could get there from Salem, Ohio, where she was living.

In later years, Josie would remember her mother saying, "Salem? That's where they sent the guns to John Brown, for his rebellion." Although she had no idea then of John Brown or his body that lay rotting in the grave, still she always associated him afterward with Margaret, and the negligible town of Salem, Ohio, which remained for her a hallowed place.

They were expecting another version of Irene—that is, a thin, wiry, dark-skinned woman—but Margaret was tall and strong with a light, freckled face and soft silvery hair, done up. Part American Indian, she told the children, and proof of that, she said, was that she always carried a forked stick, in case of snakes. She was from Mononga-hela, in the mountains, where they wished they were from. She moved into Howard and Electra's third-floor rooms, and was downstairs helping with the baby even before she unpacked.

Her wages were the going thirty dollars a week, although

a week passed, then two, with no payment. Josie's mother—Mrs. Brier, Margaret called her—asked if it would be all right "by the month," and Margaret said fine. She already knew that there was no money in that house, but knew too that Lora's parents would come through in the end, if it came to that.

As for her, she was glad enough at this particular juncture for the roof over her head. Salem had gone bad for her, once the old woman she was working for there had died and her son and his wife had moved into the old house. Both drinkers, especially the wife, who'd accused her, twice, of stealing her jewelry. What every domestic lives in fear of, and that had to be a sin, "deadly," Margaret considered it, the accusation itself—and of course they'd found the bracelet and then an earring, which the woman had dropped in the hallway, on her drunken way upstairs, and they'd apologized, or the man had, but she'd quit after the second time. Too risky.

But she hadn't found another live-in job there, just day work, and her money was running out, not to mention having to share a bedroom in the only Black rooming house in town. So Irene's call had come as a lifeline, or at least a change of luck, and when she saw the nice house and met the nice woman and children, and figured out what was going on, that pity and sorrow were called for as well as housekeeping, she felt she was the right person in the right place. Safety for her. Comfort for them.

Even if the husband did come to his senses and move back in—which he wouldn't. She knew that during her first week on the job, when he finally showed up. But it turned out that what he'd come for were some shoes he'd left—golf shoes, no less. He gave the kids some toys he'd picked up in the hospital gift shop—Teddy bears with "Get Well Quick" tags he hadn't even bothered to pull off—and hugged them, looking at his watch.

Didn't leave any money either. As for Margaret, she was glad enough to see his back. She knew his kind. Cheating men, lying men, smiling to the world, snarling to their wives. She'd had one of them herself for a while, although with her there'd never been any games about the money. She made it, he spent it, until she finally put him out the door, which had cost her. Since she'd loved him, had married him. And when he came back the first time, she'd said okay—there were her three boys still at home, the last one his, but he was nice to all three. And he loved her, he swore it, he'd missed her so much, and he had a job, and she'd believed it for a while—it was true for a while, but then, so it went, just like this. Another woman, same story, minus the big house and a maid being owed money.

Not to mention food—this guy, a doctor no less, could give the worst of them lessons. Her first week with them, there was still a chicken in the freezer in the basement, and some hamburger meat, but nothing had come in since then.

There was spaghetti in the pantry, so she cooked it up with the last of the canned tomatoes from the garden, and, when they were gone, cooked it with just margarine and salt, once even the box of Kraft cheese was empty.

But then she spotted the wooden crates in the cellar, filled with empty soda pop bottles that Golden Age Beverages had been delivering on a monthly basis for the doctor's parties. Though the deliveries had been canceled, the last crates of empties hadn't been picked up, and Margaret suggested to Lora that they haul them up the cellar stairs, and exchange them at the local market for more spaghetti, and bread and peanut butter. Luckily their milk was still being delivered. But that bill was probably about to come due.

Margaret understood why Lora didn't go to her parents, didn't want to unmask her husband as the no-good, no-'count he was.

Margaret understood this, this attempt to save what couldn't be saved. She'd seen her in his dressing room, looking through what was left, some shirts, pants, shoes. But old ones—nothing he'd want. Just stuff he'd left for her to box up, give away.

Maybe to Sim, the handyman, whose church Margaret planned on attending one of these days. Soon as she got her strength back from Salem and felt like getting out of bed early and walking all the way downtown, since the buses in this neighborhood didn't run on Sundays.

— IV —

BISHOP MAGUIRE

Martin Brier hadn't wanted to go by, but he'd needed his shoes. He had managed to slip enough of his clothes out, little by little, but the shoes had proven more difficult, sitting out there on those shelves. Visible, no dodging. He'd even considered just replacing them, but there were some good ones, and the golf shoes too, specially made for his feet, which were narrow, and he had a game later that afternoon.

So there was no help for it, but he'd still been hoping to avoid a scene. Arrive with the children napping, and maybe her too, and then have the door answered by someone he could smile at and dispatch upstairs to get the shoes.

Luckily he'd stopped in the hospital gift shop, because when he walked in the door, it was Josie who'd come bounding down the stairs, shouting through the house, "Daddy's

31

home!" Worst-case scenario. It was all he could do not to cut and run.

She was dancing around him, shouting, and of course he'd picked her up, kissed her, told her to be quiet, she'd wake the baby, but then an older woman—the new maid, he assumed—had come in with the baby, who was smiling, though the woman looked like carved stone. He'd smiled at her, but she'd just nodded—who the hell was she? Could he fire her, right then? As master of the house?

"Where's Mrs. Brier?" he asked, although that was the last thing he wanted to know. He'd hoped, in fact, not to know, though she too had come in, along with Willie, who also ran to him, and started clambering up his legs—so here was the whole nine yards. She looked like hell—tired, worn-out, and when had she last been to the hairdresser? God, who could blame him, leaving?

Josie ran and hugged her too—"Mommy, Daddy's home!"

Couldn't they all just go outside, away, leave him alone for five minutes? What about the maid, standing there, straight, unsmiling, as tall as he was, holding the baby, glaring? What was she there for? Could he order her upstairs, to pack his bag for him?

Josie was hugging him, clinging. He shook her off, nicely though, and gave her and Willie the teddy bears he'd brought, but they barely looked at them, just kept at him—

"Daddy!"—and then followed him upstairs. He turned to Lora—but she was just standing there, trying to smile. With that uncurled hair—what was she thinking?

He should have forgotten the golf game and come by late at night, obviously. He pulled down a suitcase from his closet—a good one. Dark green leather. A gift from Lora's father's cousin in California, the rich one who'd wanted to give him a job after the war. What if he'd accepted it? Another life, he guessed.

Though how different would it have been? It wasn't as if he'd have stayed in love with her there, but not here. Might have been even worse, if he'd been working for her cousin. He started throwing his shoes into the case. He should have brought something else, a paper bag. Well, he'd return this next time. It had her initials, not his.

He looked up, straight into Josie's eyes, which were on his face, searching. Gray, almost blue, like his. He smiled at her, told her he wished he had more time. She nodded gravely, her eyes never leaving his face.

He hated that—what was she looking for? Searching him, as if she were the police. Was she going to pat him down? Search the suitcase?

The shoes were packed. "Daddy loves you," he said, glancing around—had he left anything? It looked good. Whatever he'd left was left. He had to get out of here, pronto.

He picked Josie up, carried her downstairs, told her some things they were going to do together—the circus, the amusement park, the rides, cotton candy.

But no smile. "Are you coming home tonight?" she asked him. The Grand Inquisitor.

"Yes, but very late"—a lie.

She nodded—did she know? Did she have a lie detector?

The maid was there with the baby, who smiled at him.

"Cute," he said, chucking him under the chin. He tried again with the woman, said how glad they were to have her, but she was still deaf and blind.

Not that she wasn't seeing—she was seeing it all. And the worst part, she was thinking just then, was that she'd seen some photos of a party they'd had here, not even a year ago, and he'd looked really happy—he was really happy. With his wife, with his children, his friends and their children, even the old folks. His own father hanging back, having a joke with Alonzo Wilson.

It was a dream of success, of happiness. He was smiling in the photos, the picture of a man who had won the war for America, and reaped in return what the country had to offer. The wife, the children, a great career, a big house, friends, family—but there was a demon, she knew now, in the depths of him, whispering in his ear, and he was leaving it all as wreckage in his wake.

"Daddy'll be back," he'd said to Josie as he left, fled, really, and she'd nodded, silent now. No more "Daddy's home!"—thank God.

It was tough, on him too, that joy. Painful. For him too, for chrissakes! He should have just left the shoes, walked away from them, he saw that now.

Josie was standing at the door, looking down. Willie too. Why didn't they go out back and play? He'd kissed them both—what more did they want from him? Watching him like that—who'd put them up to it? Lora? His mother-in-law, whom he cordially hated? Was Josie starting to look like her?

"Be good for Daddy." He didn't add anything about helping their mother—he wasn't even thinking about their mother. He was thinking about the appointment he had now—he checked his watch—with Bishop Maguire. There was a chance he could resolve things, or at least find a way to cut some of the knots, fast, which in this case was key.

There had never been any talk about a baby, about marriage even—since he was already married and she was Catholic. But it had happened, and now she had gone and spoken to Bishop Maguire, and the idea seemed to be that he could get his first marriage, his current marriage, annulled. Since Lora wasn't Catholic—all he had to do was turn Catholic himself, which was fine with him, if it would get him out of this mess.

"Like Henry VIII," he'd joked to one of his friends. Another doctor.

"Actually, the opposite of Henry VIII," the guy had said. Meaning the Catholic part, but his point was that it had got rid of his wife.

And if this annulment worked, he might not even have to get a real divorce, with the lawyers and the money. Although it might be tricky, to get married, legally, again without it, but on the other hand, it wasn't as if he were as keen on that as she was. Still, there was probably no way out. She was a secretary, but part of the hospital staff, worked for the president of the hospital, in fact, so could be said to hold his career cupped in her pale little hands.

Which was what had drawn him in the first place—she was one of those dark redheads, tall and thin, unlike his wife, who was dark and not so tall, not the long-legged, tall, thin type he now knew was what he had been looking for all along.

He sat with her, together in Bishop Maguire's office, who allowed that there might be a case for annulment, since his current marriage hadn't been blessed in the holy Catholic Church.

"Which makes her children illegitimate," she said, "right?"

He turned to her sharply. He hadn't thought of that, though obviously she had. She had on the kind of dress he hadn't seen her in before, loose, flowing. Of course. Wouldn't want to be flaunting things to the bishop, though he'd probably seen it before in this room, plenty.

"So they're illegitimate, right?" she said again. He found those extra "rights" annoying. A little bit tough. A little bit street girl.

Although that was what he'd liked about her, right?

The bishop cleared his throat, said it would depend. Since there was a chance that they could have them baptized too, his children, and that would naturally be their goal, not cutting them off from the tree of the Church, and so on.

He stopped listening then, since that would never happen—his children, his wife's children, being baptized by Bishop Maguire. But as for the rest, he just needed the details. She wasn't showing, at least to the unpracticed eye. But some of the nurses at the hospital would have taken in the early signs, though he didn't think the gossip had spread yet. Either way, they didn't have much longer. He apparently needed a baptismal certificate for this procedure to proceed, and how long would that take?

The bishop asked if he'd completed his instruction in the Catholic faith, and with whom.

She stepped in for him. "Father Lindy says he's almost done."

A lie. He was impressed. She was good, his street girl. Tall, red-headed, and a good liar.

Well, then, said the bishop, all that was left was his baptism, which Father Lindy could perform when he finished the instruction, and then they could move forward. The letter to his current wife would go out shortly.

"Letter?"

"A matter of form. She has the right to contest," said the bishop.

He hadn't known that she'd be brought into this. Thought somehow they could do it all around her, behind her back, so that she wouldn't have to know. Since it was church, not state.

Though what difference could it make to her, what Bishop Maguire and the local Catholic See thought of her anyway? It wasn't as if their paths would ever cross.

Still, it was too bad there had to be that letter, but maybe she wouldn't contest—what was there to contest anyway? The only question was whether they'd been married in the Catholic Church, and they hadn't. Nothing to contest about that.

The problem was he hadn't told her that he was leaving, not in so many words. True, he hadn't been home lately, hadn't even remembered to send her some money, though he'd meant to. Had to, and would, later today.

But meanwhile, he realized that since everything would come out when she got the letter from the Catholics, he'd better get to the bank, quickly. Her parents had put down the money to buy the house, rather than the bank, and now his plan was to go down to the Union National, while he was still the owner, still Lora Brier's husband in the eyes of the world and the bank, and take out a mortgage against it. Since he had to buy another house, for this one—urgently. She had managed to get a room in unmarried nurses' housing at the hospital.

She told him she'd found something on the South Side, where he didn't know anyone, which was a good idea, until the dust settled. Nothing grand, just a perfectly nice three-bedroom brick, with a yard, front and back. Not too far from a park where she could walk the baby.

It was ten thousand dollars, which he could get this afternoon. With his earnings, he'd be able to pay it back before anyone noticed. She, Lora, his wife—former wife, soon to be—always left their finances to him.

He drove straight there, from Bishop Maguire's little office. Glad to be out of there—all those statues, the Virgin Marys, the Jesuses. He'd almost started humming, "*I don't care if it rains or freezes, long as I got my plastic Jesus—*" had barely caught himself, and then had to stifle a laugh.

And here he was, turning Catholic. Seeking salvation there, though maybe not the kind Bishop Maguire had in mind. He pulled up outside of the bank and went in. The managing director came to meet him with an outstretched hand. He'd just helped the guy's son get into med school. The man ushered him into his office.

— V —

LO

It was less the fact that they'd had spaghetti every night for a few weeks than the two letters she'd gotten, one from the bank about a mortgage on the house, and the other from the Catholic diocese, that sent Lora over to her parents' house again for supper. She took Margaret along, to get her some decent food too. Margaret would probably tell Irene, but the time for hiding what still felt like a personal disgrace was probably over now.

She'd been planning to wait till after dinner to break the news, but as they sat down, both children cried out, "Steak!" and both parents turned the same puzzled face to her. It was 1957. Steak wasn't a big deal in houses like theirs.

She opened her mouth to make some excuse, but couldn't think of what to say, and after a beat, her parents turned to the children, cutting their food, asking about school. Josie was tallest in her class, and the fastest runner. Willie, four, jumped up to show them how fast he could run in his Red Ball Jets. Timmy sat in his high chair and ate a potato.

After dinner, they went into the living room, and her father got down on the floor in his suit and played horsey with the children. They were delighted, but Lora knew why he'd done it. Kept her own smile, while evading her mother's eyes. Then Margaret and Irene came in and collected the children for ice cream in the kitchen, and Lora pulled Bishop Maguire's letter from her handbag.

As her father read the letter, threatening annulment along with a concomitant illegitimization of the children, his face turned pale, then red. "I didn't know," he said slowly.

Lora's eyes were on the rug—an ugly old thing, brownish, with one of those black key patterns. No one would ever accuse her mother of having good taste. Unlike her husband and Molly Waldhorn—the rugs in their house were lovely. Carpets, really. Good wool.

Her father got to his feet. "This is nothing," he said to Lora, "less than nothing." He folded the letter, put it in his pocket, asked his wife to get him one of the boxes of Whitman's Samplers that she kept on hand for her card games. He was going to pay a call on his old friend Judge Battista, down the street.

L ora's mother came back into the room, and sat down for a moment, then got up again and went out. Maybe to get the children. That was good, since Lora felt that at that very moment she couldn't handle . . . anything. No tears, no pity, no hugs, no questions. She had no answers, wouldn't even know what to lie about. For her sake, or even for his, in case he'd just temporarily taken leave of his senses, was having some sort of nervous breakdown—wasn't that more likely? Than to sic Bishop Maguire on her?

That's why she hadn't wanted to tell her parents. Wanted to hold on till the fine, clear morning that he awoke and rose up and looked around for them, his beloveds. Her, the wife he'd taken and sworn to love, and them, his three children with his light eyes and lovely little faces. She believed in that day. He would come home to his house, look around like a man back from a long voyage or captivity, touch their faces, walk through the spacious rooms, sit in his tweed armchair in the library, or the old green leather one he'd picked out. Take a pipe from his stand, a present from a patient, a music box that revolved while playing "Auld Lang Syne." They had laughed about that. They would laugh again.

And then he would stand together with her, in the back doorway, looking out over the lawn they'd put in and that

she was still watering faithfully. She would be tempted then
to tell him that she knew, she had known, and how she'd
gotten through, what she'd summoned to keep the faith—
but she wouldn't. He didn't like her to talk. He didn't like
to listen. He just liked her to be there, and that's what she
would do. Just be there. Stand beside him, with his arm
around her, and maybe one around their daughter, and he
would look out and say something funny, call to Will, let
him run fast for him, jump around, ride his little bike. He
would kiss the baby.

She hadn't shown her father the letter from the bank.
That was just the bank, not the Spanish Inquisition. She
was still thinking that maybe she could go in the morning
with Mr. Crow, her father's lawyer. Swear him to secrecy,
lawyer-style, so her father wouldn't find out and hold it
against her husband, if—when—he came back.

Margaret came out of the kitchen with the children. The
baby had fallen asleep, it was time to go. Her father wasn't
back, but what was the point of waiting? What could he say
that would really help? That Judge Battista had ordered her
husband to love her?

"Dad will call in the morning," said her mother as they
left. She told her not to worry, it would be fine, and pressed
forty dollars into her hand. "Just until this is sorted," she

said, and bent to kiss the children, but Lora stepped away. If her mother touched her right then, she was afraid she'd fall sobbing at her feet.

She didn't sleep that night—though she must have, because she dreamt that Bishop Maguire had come to the house and caught her downstairs in her nightgown, the filmy one she hated and hardly ever wore. But she had it on for some reason, and it was clinging to her breasts, her pubic hair, and he could see everything, he was looking at her with disgust, contempt. A woman with breasts and a crotch, all showing, all disgusting. That was why she had to be annulled.

She awoke with the covers thrown off—the heavy bedspread. She should have folded it over the chaise, like Electra did, and Margaret, when she had time. It was late—where were the children? Josie must be at school. She went into the bathroom, but decided not to wash her face, so as to steer clear of the mirror. She knew what she looked like. She'd seen herself in the dream.

And the point now was to get out of her nightgown, quickly—even though it was solid cotton, not the filmy one. But still, she needed clothes, armor, protection. Pants and a jacket, so no one could see. She started toward the closet, but then there, in the laundry basket, were her jeans—the old red ones that she used for gardening. Perfect, she realized. Covered with dirt from the digging, but that was good, it would add a layer. There was nothing see-through about dirt, and the jeans had gotten big on her now, since the baby. She'd worn them almost through the pregnancy.

Her friendly old red jeans that she loved. No one could see anything through those jeans, not even the Spanish Inquisition, though there was the bank, she suddenly remembered—no red jeans there, but she would leave the bank for later. Maybe he would change his mind, put the money back, and then she wouldn't have to go. That would be best. All she had to do was give him time.

And there were her old saddle shoes, from high school. More old friends. See, world? She still had friends. Her husband might be on the loose, walking out, leaving her as if she herself were old jeans and muddy shoes. He might be calling out both the financial and ecclesiastical powers of the realm against her, but she too had friends at hand, right here, in her closet.

She needed breakfast, she was thinking, although she wasn't sure what they had. Oatmeal, maybe still? Some milk? But then she saw her mother's forty dollars on the bureau. Another friend! She would go to the market, get some coffee, yes, just what she needed! And lots of food, cereal, bread, hamburger, everything. Butterscotch sauce. Peanut butter for the children. Grape jelly.

Margaret tried to get her to drink a cup of something as she was leaving, but she was through with drinking "something." Postum or whatever it was, some cheap substitute. She was going to get coffee, she told her. She would be right back.

"Are you feeling all right, Mrs. Brier?" Margaret asked her.

"Yes, fine, perfect," she said. "I just need some coffee."

"We can call the market," Margaret said, but Lora didn't want to call, she wanted to get it, right away, there was much they had to do. Make dinner, for example, in case he came home tonight. Which was likely.

"Mrs. Brier," said Margaret.

"What?"

Margaret looked worried, but maybe Margaret was a worrier. She, Lora, wasn't going to worry now. She was almost sure he would be coming home this very night. She leaned over to kiss the baby—he put his dirty little hands on her shirt.

What was it? Ketchup? But what did that matter? The shirt was dirty already. Her favorite old flannel—she'd worn it last week, for something, the garden. What had she been doing last week? Painting? Going through boxes? A while ago, before . . . all this.

As she was leaving, Margaret tried to give her her raincoat, but it wasn't raining. Why should she wear her raincoat? She hugged Willie and said she'd be right back, and drove to the market for some coffee.

And food, of course, she told Mr. Sacker, who looked a bit—what? Off? Surprised? He asked if she was all right. She said yes, obviously she was all right, she had forty dollars in her pocket—but why had he asked? Did she look like a woman in a filmy nightgown? Different from the other women in there, buying chicken, hamburger, sliced cheese, and cans of tomato soup? Women whose husbands weren't trying to annul them? She too was buying hamburger and tomato soup, just like the rest of them, plus the coffee and even canned peaches—but could he tell? Had he heard?

He was such a gossip, Mr. Sacker. The thing was, and she almost told him, that when she looked at the letter again, she saw that her name had been misspelled. "Laura," not "Lora." Bishop Maguire had gotten it wrong. Ha, ha, "Wrong Laura," she could claim, and prove it with her driver's license, if they came to take her to the stake with their cart.

Although it was strange, almost hurtful, that he, her husband, hadn't told them how to spell her name. Especially since he knew it bothered her, plagued her, this idiosyncratic spelling she'd been saddled with, for what should have been a simple American name.

"It's European," her mother always insisted about the spelling, but from what country, might she ask? French was Laure, German was Laura, just like English, which was presumably the language her great-grandmother was speaking when she gave Lora's aunt the name, spelled, for no rational reason, Lora. That Lora, said to be the most beautiful of the sisters, had blond curls and blue eyes, but still had died in New York at age sixteen, of strep throat, went the story—but since it was around 1918, wouldn't it have been Spanish flu? Not that it mattered. What mattered was that she had died, but her name lived on, to be misspelled by these local Inquisitors, hoping to burn her namesake at the stake.

But the misspelling should cancel the whole thing anyway, so, as her father had said, why worry? And was her husband really trying to get his marriage to her annulled? What had he told the bishop? That his marriage to her was unconsummated? That his children were actually the milkman's?

How could he have, or maybe he hadn't? She stopped in the middle of the aisle. Now that she thought about it, it was obvious. He hadn't.

First of all, he would have spelled her name right. Obviously. It must have been some woman, trying to entrap him, who had gone there on her own and lied and cheated. He had probably told her that he was coming back to her, Lora, his lawful wedded wife. That he loved her, just as he had sworn to love her when he'd begged her to run away with him, when she was barely eighteen, and he was shipping out to the South Pacific. She was enrolled in college—she had other boyfriends, although no one like him. She had never really kissed a boy till him. It was 1942. He was a naval officer, irresistible in a white uniform with white gloves, and she hadn't resisted, couldn't resist, had stood in front of a judge and gone with him to a hotel room instead of to her dorm in Bloomington, Indiana, to study dramatic arts. Her passion.

Former passion, for now she was married—legally, even if it wasn't by a Catholic priest, but they weren't Catholic anyway, and she had turned eighteen, so of age, it was all on the up-and-up, she even had the marriage license somewhere, though she'd lost the ring—actually, she'd thrown it into Lake Erie. The first time she found out about . . . she didn't remember who. A nurse, after the war, when he was in medical school, but soon after that, she was pregnant with Josie. And he'd sworn it was nothing, he didn't know what had come over him, it was the war, he was sorry, he loved her, and then he loved the child, Josie, and then the next two, both boys, he was thrilled, he "had it all," she had heard him say, more than once, and he loved them, loved the house, even loved the dog he'd gotten. A dalmatian that Josie had named Straw Hat.

He probably didn't even know about the letter from the bishop—of course! He couldn't know. Not only that, but the other day, when he'd come to get his shoes, there had been that one moment, when he'd raised his hand to his eyebrow, and half smiled, half frowned, like he used to. Sweetly, like he used to. When he'd left that cold, stiff stranger he'd become, just for a moment, and gone back to himself, the man who loved her.

Just for a moment, she'd admit, and he wasn't really looking at her, but still, there he was, the real him. And then he'd bent down for something, the way he bent, with the grace, ease, a sort of joy in life that was always there, around him, and now, as she called back that bad scene in the bedroom, she realized she had missed that somehow. That bit of proof that he still loved her, had to, or that little smile wouldn't have crossed his face.

She left her cart in the middle of the aisle, gave Mr. Sacker the forty dollars, asked him to deliver, please, and rushed out of the market. She had to get to his office, had to tell him. He had to know, had to make some calls. Stop this whole nightmare, and then he had to hold her in his arms, and tell her it was okay, all a mistake, and that he would be home again soon, that very night.

The receptionist looked surprised to see her, but why was she surprised? This was Dr. Brier's office, she was Dr. Brier's wife!

The woman had looked around, alarmed almost—but at what? Because her hair wasn't combed? Had she forgotten her lipstick? So what? True, she didn't usually come by his office in old red jeans and a shirt smeared with ketchup, but it wasn't as if she'd shown up in the nightgown.

"Dr. Brier isn't here."

"You're lying!" Because he had to be there—there were patients filling all the chairs in the waiting room. They must have appointments. "Don't you?" Lora turned to them. They all looked at each other, and then away.

"Don't you have appointments?" No answer. She raised her voice. "You didn't come here just for fun, did you?"

Betty came out, from the back. Knock-kneed, buck-toothed Betty, who'd come to their housewarming, nice Betty who'd knitted a little sweater for the baby. She said hello nicely, took Lora's hand, led her to the door, and explained that Dr. Brier had had "an emergency." He was at the hospital.

"Here, let me help you." Betty took her arm and led her outside.

Was she helping her? Knock-kneed, bucktoothed, skinny Betty with her short, wispy, mousy hair—looking back over her shoulder, pushing Lora out the door, holding her arm, walking her across the parking lot, still in her thin white uniform. Her ugly white shoes.

Betty was ugly too. Lora had never let herself say it, or even think it before. She looked at her face, her eyes. Betty was frowning, worried, even scared—for what, though?

Was she in love with him?

That thought hadn't crossed Lora's mind till then. But if she was—had Betty been the one, then, who'd gone to the bishop and lied? Was it possible that Betty had even dreamt that Lora's husband would leave her for Betty?

Whatever it was, there was no further time to waste.

"Let me drive you home," Betty was saying, but Lora wasn't going home.

"Go back to work," she told Betty. An order, just in case she forgot who was Dr. Brier's wife here. She got into her car and locked the door. She would drive over to the hospital and find him, the sooner the better now, and tell him what she'd figured out. Because he would be so glad to know, he would be grateful. To find out that someone had forged his name to the bishop and then do something about it—and at the bank too. Of course. It all was falling into place.

She started her car, but then another car was pulling out of the lot, just like his—was it him? How could that be? If he was at the hospital? So Betty was lying too, on top of her other crimes? She pulled up behind him.

There was someone in the car—a nurse? A patient? She honked her horn, so he would see her, stop, get out, come talk to her, explain. And she would tell him about the letter, and the bank, and he would stop everything, fix it all. Go to the bishop and the bank that morning.

But he must not have seen her, and instead of stopping, he pulled out, fast, into traffic. She honked again. The woman turned around, then her head disappeared. Was she hiding? Had she seen her? Had he? But then why didn't he stop?

She drove after him, speeding up as he did. She would catch him, and then when he came over to her car, she would get out and kiss him on the lips, their kind of kiss, deep and slow, and push herself against him. He loved that, he would remember how much, once she got close to him. Once he smelled her—he loved her smell. He told her that, over and over. She loved his too. A deep clean evergreen scent, from way inside him.

He was driving so fast. Where were they going? The South Side? She wasn't sure, just followed, foot on the gas, eyes front. The woman must still be in the car, hiding, on the seat or the floor—was this possible? Someone so low, so common, to be hiding in a man's car from his wife?

He finally came to a stop on a small dead-end street. She pulled up behind him, and ran over to his car, so he could get out and take her in his arms, but he didn't. Didn't even turn to look at her, just sat there, staring straight ahead.

Didn't he see her? She called his name.

"Did you know about the letter? From Bishop Maguire? Did they tell you?"

Nothing. He just sat there, eyes front, hands on the steering wheel, as if he'd been turned to stone or glass, under some spell, and couldn't hear her. As if she'd already been annulled.

But she wasn't annulled, she was there, in the flesh, his lawful, wedded wife. Was he crazy? Drugged? She started pounding on the window—"Did you hear what they did at the bank? Do you even know?"

If he'd just open the door, even a little, she could wake him up from this nightmare, shatter the glass that had come down between them, all around them, and it would be over. He would shake his head, take her in his arms, smile, and everything would be all right again—when had he last smiled at her? If he did, then maybe it would all come back to him. She could touch his face, and he would remember—who she was, who they were. Them.

And whoever was in his car, on his floor, could get up, straighten her dress, and go back to her life, too. And everything would make sense again.

But he didn't open the window, didn't turn his head, just sat there, not moving, no matter how hard she pounded and begged him, until finally—she wasn't sure what happened. She must have slipped, fallen, because she was lying on the road and remembered afterward thinking that he might start up his car and drive over her. Which would solve everything, in its way.

Or maybe he would call the men in the little white coats to come and take her to Woodside with the rest of the nervous-breakdown types, and that too would be a solution. At least, for her immediate problem of how to get up and back into her car, where she would have to sit with two hands on the wheel, and turn the key, release the brake, and back down the street, as if she were a regular woman with a husband who was coming home that night, instead of a reject, an outcast, who had fallen in the dirt after baying like a crazy woman, at the window of the car where her husband was sitting with a new girlfriend, and what would they do, once they were rid of her, right then? Would he help her back up onto the seat, maybe brush her off, with apologies and concern, would they turn to each other and take a deep breath? Maybe even start to laugh, first the slutty woman, and then her husband? Whom she loved?

"Oh, Mrs. Brier, the good Lord makes our shoulders broad enough to bear whatever cross he lays upon them," was what Margaret said later, after she had finally, somehow, driven home and walked in the door. She, Margaret, was in the kitchen, the baby in her arms. The children were in the playroom. Lora steadied herself, took a breath. Groped her way to the breakfast room table and sat down.

Josie came to give her a hug and then stopped. "What happened, Mommy?" She was staring at her knee.

Lora looked down. Her pants were torn, her old red jeans. She hadn't realized.

"Nothing, sweetie, Mommy slipped on the ice"—but there wasn't any ice. It was spring. April. She turned to Margaret.

"The groceries, I must have left them—"

But Margaret said Mr. Sacker had brought them by, and she was making some soup and hamburgers for the children. "Let's go upstairs," said Margaret, and they must have, because she found herself first in the bath, and then in bed. Margaret brought her some tea or soup or something, and she must have drunk it, and then fallen asleep, because when she finally woke up, it was morning.

The two older children had crawled into bed with her. The bed was enormous—one of the new king-sized ones, that he'd wanted. Molly Waldhorn had to have the bedspread specially made, and asked for her monogram, but he wanted his initials on it too. Molly Waldhorn had raised an eyebrow, but just a little. He was the one paying, and she knew he'd come from nothing. He was allowed some leeway. All her clients were.

The baby started calling, from the next room. Would she get up and go to him, or wouldn't she? That was the question. She could stay in bed, call Margaret. Stay in bed for a week, or the rest of the year. *She has a right,* she could hear them all saying. *Her husband leaving her like that. Of course she's in bed, poor thing.*

Would they wonder why, though—not that she was in bed, but that he'd left? Think back on missteps they might remember, school days, summers, skating on the pond? She'd been a star, always—A's in school, leading roles in the plays. Maybe it would be less missteps than comeuppance. Her friends were less pretty, less smart, but who were the ones with the husbands in bed beside them? Lora with the fancy spelling or Sally, Phyllis, Jean?

She got up. She would get up. That was how she would do it. On her feet, not in bed. When she picked up the baby, she couldn't stop the tears from falling on his little face, but he didn't seem to notice, just smiled up at her. Good to know, she thought. Maybe the world paid less attention than one thought. Feared.

She smiled down at him. Breathed in and breathed out. "Mommy," called Willie, from her bed.

She might not be "darling" to her husband anymore, or even Mrs. Brier for much longer, but she was still "Mommy." That wouldn't change.

"Be right there with Tootles," she answered. That's what

they called the baby. They all loved him—"*soooo much,*" she sang, and hugged him.

Another breath. Okay.

"Here's the little guy!" She put him on the bed with the other two. They started to play with the pillows.

She went into the bathroom, washed her face, though didn't look at herself in the mirror. She had to stop crying, had to get out of bed, had to look with love upon the children, tell them stories, sit at dinner, and take them places in the car. But she didn't have to look in the mirror right now, and she wouldn't.

Her father came by that afternoon, searched her face, and gave her a brief hug. She couldn't remember the last time he'd hugged anyone over the age of seven. Judge Battista had called Bishop Maguire to remind him of the precedence of civil marriage in the United States of America. Maguire had apologized and explained that he had not been apprised of all the facts in the case.

She listened to her father, thinking mostly that she was just glad that she'd gotten out of bed. He looked worried enough as it was. He had begged her not to get married, to wait, to go to college and then see. He hadn't liked her husband, even as the children were born. He'd probably heard rumors—something, anyway. The early whispers.

And now she, who had insisted on the marriage, she who hadn't listened, was not only proving him right but bringing disgrace upon them all. There had never been a divorce in their family, or even among their friends. Divorce was something they read about in the newspapers—movie stars. Profligate heiresses living in Europe. People with no roots and no grounding. No one they knew.

Her father said that Bishop Maguire had mentioned to Judge Battista that her husband was planning to remarry, "after he converted."

She looked up, shocked. Truly shocked, as much by the "converted" as the "remarry."

"He didn't tell you?"

She just shook her head, couldn't meet his eyes. She felt like she was the one who'd been caught out, somehow. Revealed. Subject to shame.

"Has he asked for a divorce?"

Another silent no. He hadn't faced it, or her. He'd just had Howard sneak his clothes out, she could see that now. And even when he'd found himself compelled to come by the house to get his shoes, he still hadn't said a word.

Although in his defense, she'd kept out of his way that day, in the hopes that he'd linger a bit with the children, hug them, and look in on the baby. But he hadn't, just brushed off Josie and Will with his usual "Daddy's really busy now," and made off with his suitcase—her suitcase—

without a look back at the two stricken faces. Three, if you counted hers.

She still wasn't ready, though, to tell her father all this, to let him take full measure of this man whom she still—it was true—loved. Was still prepared to shield.

Her father asked if she would consider a reconciliation, if someone could talk sense to him. A friend, one of the doctors, someone older.

Would she? She had a flash vision of herself in a hat. A sensible suit, chairing a meeting. The Ladies' Auxiliary. Friends of the Library. Butler Art. She knew these women—just hadn't known what it signified. Those tight faces. The martinis at lunch. Always making a point of their names—Mrs. John Jones. Never Judy.

But now she got it, the whole essence of the thing, what lay beneath. Damned right they were going to use those names. The whole charade was being played out to keep their names—in her case, "Mrs. Martin Brier." Because who would she be without it? Lora Elgar, her girlhood name? Virginal, maidenly, seventeen, at home?

But she was thirty now, and that cage had been flown, joyfully, willingly, and yes, willfully, when he came into her life one day and called her "Lo." Not "Lor," as her brothers and friends did, not "Lora," like her parents and teachers, but "Lo." She'd taken flight on that name—"Lo." So free suddenly, with no *r* at the end to ground her. *Lo*, he'd whispered into her hair, her ear, as no boy had ever whispered before. And then he'd kissed her, his way, and she was overcome, her whole body, arms and legs, she was Lo, his love.

"Marry me," he'd whispered, and it was yes—what else was there for him from her in this life but yes?

He'd called her Lora, though, the last time they'd spoken. Lo was gone, and in answer to her father's question—"Did he ask for a divorce?"—she could have said, *Yes, he called me Lora*, and gone on to explain that rather than his beloved Lo, she was now the madwoman in his attic, the dog in his manger, the crazed harridan pounding on his window in old red jeans, whose shrieks had sent his new Lo cowering at his feet.

She was Lora to him now, she might have explained to her father, ice-cold, not even "Lor." She was Lora, her formal legal name, though he'd tried to strip her of that too, the Mrs. Brier part. Ecclesiastically, but what had he been thinking? That having cast her out, the whole of the established patriarchy would go along with him? That she had no father with lawyer and judge friends to marshal the law of the land against Rome?

So now he would have to revert to the U.S. courts, but since he hadn't yet, as far as she knew, in answer to her father's question about reconciliation—would she? could she?— she'd answered, "Maybe, for the children."

Since there was a chance that he'd come back, once he

realized that it would have to be a serious divorce, no slippy-slidey Catholic side deal, and that would hurt him too. His reputation, his standing at the hospital, in the community—especially once her father and brothers took a public stand against him. By marrying her, he'd taken his place in their world, but that world would close ranks against him now. There'd be no more cottages on the lake with her friends, no more Christmas parties at the big house on Fifth Avenue. No membership in the country club that he'd been excited to join.

Had he thought about that? That he'd be back to golf at Muni? If someone laid it out for him that way, might he reconsider? And then she'd be Mrs. Martin Brier, club woman, whose husband didn't love her, but never mind. She was not divorced, not a divorcée, she was Mrs. Martin Brier, whatever that would come to mean.

Separate bedrooms? Dinners? Vacations? And the children—what would they grow up seeing? But at least they'd have a father. A mother who was Mrs. Martin Brier.

She thought of what she would say to him, what she could say. There were three children vs. the two of them, so their marital happiness mattered less, weighed less, so to speak, than the children's overall well-being? Or she could mention his parents, how much this marriage had meant to them, and how much they loved the children, even the house. His mother especially would be devastated.

But she wasn't sure he cared particularly about his parents. A few months ago, when they'd come by one evening, he hadn't let them in the door. She'd been upstairs, with the children, and when she heard the bell and started down, he'd motioned to her angrily, almost violently.

Josie came running up. "It's Nana!"

He grabbed her arm, held her back. "Quiet! We're hiding!"

"From Nana?"

"Just for fun." He picked her up. "It's a game."

"Is Nana playing too?"

But Nana wasn't playing, she was standing there, with a box in her hands—probably some of her special cookies that she'd made for them. She rang again. They could see her, through the windowpanes in the door, first hesitating on the doorstep another moment, then turning and walking slowly back to the car, where her husband was waiting. He wasn't the visiting type.

"Nana was coming to see us," said Josie, looking at her father, puzzled. She didn't look at Lora. As if she already knew.

"I'm exhausted," he said, and the child had nodded. And thinking back to this, Lora wondered if it would be worth it after all, any desperate ploy to save the marriage. Because it had chilled her, the way he'd left his mother standing on the doorstep, the door closed in her face. Both cars were there, in the garage behind the house, for his mother to see. She must have known. Otherwise she would have rung again, or even tried the front door. To leave the cookies inside for the children.

She must have known that her son hadn't opened the door to her, although she might have blamed Lora. "My daughter-in-law closed her door to me"—bitter enough in itself, but still through a glass darkly. Josie, though, had seen face-to-face.

"Were we hiding?" she asked him again, later. "From Nana?"

"Yes," he said, "for fun."

But it hadn't been fun, not for anyone, and for what? Lora wondered. Why? They could have had her in for fifteen minutes. Made some tea. She could have taken her upstairs, shown her the baby's new crib, the children would have hugged and kissed her, and she would have gone home, and it would have been nothing. But now, it was there, a permanent question: *What kind of a man?* And Josie had stood on the stairs, taking it in.

It had chilled her, Lora too, and made her wonder now if there was any way to reach him. She could still picture them together, smiling, laughing like they used to, and she could still picture herself believing what she could almost hear him saying, that this was all a mistake.

But maybe that man was gone, the one she'd laughed with. Didn't exist anymore, but still, she agreed to the letter her father had suggested, proposing a marriage in name only, "for the children." He would have his freedom. They would work it out.

She sent it to his office, but got no answer. What did come in the mail was a notarized petition for divorce.

"VOLARE"

Looking back, Lora couldn't remember how it all rolled out. She was the one with "grounds"—adultery—but he was the one wanting the divorce. With nothing left to protect, she showed her father the letter from the bank, with the shocking news that her husband had taken out a mortgage on the house he had abandoned.

Her father had rushed to the bank with Mr. Crow, the lawyer, but what they found was a fait accompli. All they could have done at that point was get the banker fired, since Lora's signature had been forged, and prosecute her husband. In either criminal or civil court, Mr. Crow was thinking.

He'd discovered that the money had gone for another house, for the pregnant girlfriend, so would be complicated to recover. But the man was clearly a scoundrel, and Mr.

Crow was all for pressing charges against "that no-good louse," as he put it to her father.

She wasn't prepared for that level of public dirty laundry, though. She let her father organize a milder legal response, which included alimony and child support, as well as repayment of the mortgage over time, to all of which her husband's lawyer quickly agreed.

"Thank God he didn't ask for joint custody!" said her mother.

"Joint custody?" That was probably the one thing in this whole nightmare that had never haunted Lora, not for a moment. This was a man who'd closed his door to his mother. Who'd told his small daughter not to breathe in his face. Who'd left her, his wife, scrabbling in the dust, pounding on his window. Who hadn't been to see his children since . . . when? When he'd run out of shoes and been forced to come home so he could prance around on the golf course in his two-tone spectators. Go out that evening in his smooth black loafers. And even then was annoyed that he'd had to bend over and kiss the children briefly and tell them his same old lie.

Not even a new one, something up-to-date for a man who was leaving them with nothing. Less than nothing— who had stolen part of their house! Joint custody indeed! She was the one who'd had to sit Josie on the green leather footstool he had ordered from Molly Waldhorn, and tell her that they were getting divorced. The child somehow knew what the word meant, and had started sobbing, pitifully, and all Lora could do was gather her in her inadequate arms. Inadequate since what the child wanted were male arms, strong arms, the ones she loved. Her father's.

But that was over. Lora knew it now. Even though his lawyer finally got around to mentioning "visitation rights," which had cheered her briefly. But she realized now that that was just another one of his charming lies. His garden full of weeds.

Worse than weeds—a briar patch, quicksand. The way his "visitations" worked was that he'd make a date to pick them up, Josie and Will, and they would get excited. Margaret would dress them in something special, matching sailor suits, and when he didn't show, she, Lora, would call his office to remind him. One of the nurses would take the message. She even told them that the children were waiting in front of the house, lest the prospect of an encounter with her was putting him off.

And there they'd be, the two children, standing waiting, for anyone driving by to see. Did he ever come? Once? Years later, she tried to remember. Occasionally his office would call to say he was coming, on his way, but they turned out to be liars too, even Betty. Collaborators, nurses serving their doctor. If she called right back, they'd let it ring. She knew by then that his new home number was unlisted—another thing they'd never heard of in that town. Something else for movie stars and gangsters.

Once Betty did call, though late, with an excuse, and ask to reschedule, and on that day, Lora and Margaret dressed the children again, but the next time, she got into her car and made an excuse, a drink with a friend, and drove away, so as to spare herself the worst of the aftermath.

But then she realized there couldn't be a drink with a friend, not yet. People were finding out, one by one. They would either be curious or overly kind, which left her with no one to talk to. Even her mother was always fighting tears these days. What she needed was someone who didn't know, who would talk to her about the weather, Adlai Stevenson, *Around the World in Eighty Days.* She drove to the park, nearby, but there were too many children playing in the creek and on the swings—children whose fathers would be home that night for supper. She started over toward the South Side, but then was stricken with the fear that she might run across them—him and her. Since she knew in her heart that he wasn't coming for the children.

She went to the gas station. That was something to do, something she needed. The boy "filled her up"—she pulled out the change. Almost two dollars—at twenty-five cents a gallon, she had needed eight gallons. Two dollars. Almost half a tank. She'd heard somewhere that gas in Europe was fifty cents—was that possible? Why couldn't she sit with someone and talk about that?

She turned on the radio—"Heartbreak Hotel." Elvis was sad too—his baby had left him. He'd found a new place to dwell. Was there room for her? What if she just drove down south and moved in there? Could she write to him and get an address?

The boy had finished, she had to move on. Drive somewhere else. Should she get something for the children, ice-cream cones? There was the Moo Shop, but no way to bring a soda home, the ones they liked, with cherry ice cream. Maybe, if he hadn't come, she could bundle them into the car and bring them back here for supper, for fun. Life with Mom.

She drove home, and was relieved that they weren't still standing outside. Had he come, then? They would be so happy, so happy—she would be so happy, just to have his warmth in their lives again. She realized then how cold it was without him. They were freezing to death.

"He came?" she called out to Margaret.

Margaret shook her head, no. She told her they'd waited outside for a while, "too long," and even at that, she'd had a hard time getting them back inside. "What if he comes?" Josie kept saying. And then they'd both stood stock-still as she got them out of their good clothes, even Willie, who never stood still. She'd made them hot chocolate and cinnamon toast, and Willie went out back to play, but Josie kept going to the window, checking. *In case he comes.*

That night, Lora and Margaret roasted weenies with them over the fire in the den, but that was when Josie started wetting her bed again. It went on for a while. She'd come into Lora's room, dripping wet, shivering, and Lora would have to wash her, change her, and in the morning Margaret would strip the bed and open the window, even though now it was winter.

"It smells like she's sick," Margaret would say, and she probably was, but the pediatrician couldn't find anything wrong. He said it was normal, it happened, and they didn't discuss why.

Though he probably knew by then. Being a doctor and in on doctors' gossip.

But everyone knew—what was she thinking? Soon afterward, she got an invoice from the bank for the mortgage he'd taken out on her house. Mr. Crow, her lawyer, assured her that she would be getting alimony and child support, but he hadn't said when, and there was no way she could meet the bank's payments. She called a realtor and started looking for a smaller house.

"It will be cozy," she told Josie. "We'll sit in front of the fire and have fun in the new house. Make popcorn.

Cuddle in bed." She realized that everything she was proffering the children spoke of warmth, of coziness, small rooms they could fill, as opposed to this spacious house, empty without him.

"But what if he comes to get us here? How will he find us?" Josie kept asking. And the real question: "When is he coming?"

Lora didn't say never, though she thought that it was possible. Possible that they no longer even crossed his mind. Could someone talk to him? Was there anyone who could get through? She'd heard from her brothers that he'd gotten a few calls from friends who'd seen the children, standing there, forlorn, waiting for him. Friends who called his office and told him to get into his car and get the hell over there, and she knew the lies he'd told them. That he was actually right then about to go get them, after some tricky medical situation he'd had to resolve, and take them to Dairy Queen, or out to Brauningers' Farm, to see the reindeer. Maybe he even believed it himself, until the time came to actually get into his car and he realized that he wasn't going after all.

He loved the children, true. Just couldn't quite deal with them right then, given his present situation. A new wife, almost, although it was taking longer, since the free and easy annulment she'd waved before him like a perfumed handkerchief had proved delusive. So he was stuck in divorce court, with a new baby coming that he hadn't actually wanted. Hadn't signed up for.

Lora knew this without being told. Would bet twenty dollars that he already wanted out. Now that it no longer mattered, she realized that she knew him, and could muster a much colder eye. She had recently found herself remembering the time she'd been taken to the opera in Cleveland, by a friend's mother, to see *Don Giovanni*. She hadn't much liked it. She had no connection to the music, no way in, and the diva was too old, too fat, and the story had seemed almost ridiculous. A talking statue. A man whose pleasure fleets at the very moment he obtains it.

Absurd, she'd thought, a fairy tale, but now she found herself wondering, looking back, if he had already tired of her on their wedding night, as Don Giovanni would have. Whereas Donna Anna, and she herself, had only fallen more deeply in love. As she got to know him, his body, his smile, his scent. His sleep. She loved all that, and when he'd shipped out again, to the South Pacific, she'd prayed, been terrified, watched for the moon every night, praying that he could see it too, that he was blessed, watched-over. He'd been on two ships that were hit, but he'd survived, somehow. And then in the summer of 1945, just as his ship was sailing for Japan, facing the prospect of decimating casualties, the atomic bomb had been dropped, and the war was over. He'd come back, safe and sound.

And gone on to medical school, and she'd worked there at the lab, to support them, a young married couple, scrimping and saving, living in a small apartment in Cleveland. Although even then, she was knowing, starting to know. She found traces, lipstick. A condom when they weren't using condoms. They were trying to have children—why didn't she leave him then? Free and clear.

She could have, obviously should have, but then he'd come home at night and tell her how much he loved her. Smile at her with his beautiful lips, his beautiful blue-gray eyes, and she thought it was true, thought it was fixed, and bigger than what was on the side, the cheap lipstick on his collar. She felt sure then, when he took her in his arms, that he did love her and, beyond that, loved the life they were planning together. A beautiful life, with a small house and then a bigger one and children and a dog and their friends. Her dream—his too, she thought.

Although once, when she was already pregnant, a girl she worked with at the med school lab mentioned that she had a date that night with a resident from out of town, a doctor. She mentioned the place. "Aren't you from there?" the girl asked her.

And she'd frozen for an instant, and then got quickly to her feet and, feigning illness, had rushed to the bathroom. She leaned against the sink there, took a few breaths, threw water on her face. She was wearing one of those ugly skirts with a hole for her pregnant stomach and a sort of smock, pastel, plaid. She didn't wear pastels, she wore red and black and white, but they didn't have maternity clothes in those colors. Was it her fault she looked like a farm girl?

Like someone he probably never would have dated, or even looked at. She took a few deep breaths, looked down at her watch, let a minute pass and then another. Enough time for the little matter, broached so lightly, about some random doctor from a small town who had chanced to invite her lab partner for dinner that night, to float off into the ether, somewhere behind her.

Because she knew which doctor as soon as the girl had posed her innocent question, but couldn't bear to hear his name said out loud. And when the phone rang in their apartment that evening on cue, she hadn't answered. She knew it was him, calling to tell her he had to work late, and she didn't want to hear that lie said out loud. She was pregnant with his child, she loved him, really loved him, although looking back, it was obvious she should have left him then. It would have been hard with a child, but less hard than with three, and she would have been twenty-five, not thirty. She could have still married one of the boys from high school who'd been in love with her. One of the boys who'd moved back after college and the war and picked up the family business.

But now they were all married, all good husbands, and here she was. Still dreaming—him coming toward her, smiling. Him calling her "Lo." But in her waking hours, she was inching toward seeing him as a man she didn't much like. Just some man—ever since that day on the steps, with his mother outside the door. She had looked into his face then and seen less beauty than strangeness. As in a stranger, with eyes that refused to meet theirs, even Josie's. He was alone there, even with the woman he'd slept in bed with for a quarter of his life and the children who'd sprung from the best of those moments.

Alone like Don Giovanni too, Lora was thinking, although this wouldn't be much consolation for the children. Couldn't someone tell him how much he meant to them, right now? That in ten years he would be less, always less, but that now he was everything?

She ran through his friends in her mind, but she couldn't picture anyone who could talk to him. Except maybe Bishop Maguire, and he'd have to save his breath for the next divorce.

Josie was having bad dreams, especially a recurring one. She was walking down their street, on their block, and their house wasn't there. She told Lora she thought maybe she was on the wrong block, and checked, but she wasn't. There were all the neighbors' houses, just not theirs.

Lora didn't need Sigmund Freud to analyze that one. She

picked up the volume of Keats that she'd been given as a prize for declamation, in tenth grade.

> *And Joy, whose hand is ever at his lips*
> *Bidding adieu; and aching Pleasure nigh,*
> *Turning to poison . . .*

True, she realized. She was making some decisions. She would start where she'd left off and go to college. Not the Indiana University of her youth and dreams of studying drama but the local college, for a teaching degree. She would go for dual certification, elementary and high school, so she'd be sure to get a job as soon as she finished. She would also approach her parents, lay out her situation, and ask them to move into the house with her and the children, so they could stay put, and Josie could stop dreaming that her house had disappeared.

She would give them the master bedroom, and move into the baby's room. The two boys could sleep together, which was fine, better even. They would be a good full six around the dinner table, better than the shivering four they were now.

And if he comes back? asked Josie.

"We can put a leaf in the table," said Lora. She kissed her.

His daughter, the last man standing, Lora found herself thinking. Absurdly, but somehow true. Sad but true.

Margaret went into the den and picked up the blocks the children had been playing with. She wasn't supposed to—it was Willie's job—but he'd gone up to play with his cowboys and horses, and forgotten. Which was fine with her. She'd observed that on nights like this, when he was able to lose himself with those cowboys, she could sing him to sleep.

But there had been a look on Josie's face, a way she'd look up and then down, her lips pursed, and then to the side, as if seeking aid, some lifeline to keep her from falling into the black hole of his absence. And then Margaret had heard her, on the phone, to the Medical Dental Bureau—how had she ever got hold of that number? He must have given it to her, in one of his gestures—one of his "You can call me any time, sweetie" moments. The women at that answering service were always nice to Josie and promised to tell her father that she'd called.

"Tell him to call me, please," Margaret heard her pleading into the phone. "Even if it's late. Mommy will wake me."

Who does this kind of thing to his children? Leave, yes; but leave like this? Strewing promises behind, keeping them half-sick with hope? Why? To keep himself believing—so he could keep telling himself, his nurses, those mornings when he'd made a date to pick them up, that he would be leaving early, taking his children to the circus that day? To the park? To supper at the Golden Drumstick or even the Mural Room? Josie loved the parfaits there for dessert, and picking out a toy from the treasure chest they kept on a little stage near the organ, for children.

He probably even smiled at the thought, of how happy she'd be. Willie too, though he could be trouble. But not Josie, never Josie, such a good child, pretty too—no wonder he loved her. It would be great to see her, it had been too long. Good that he was going to pick her up.

And it would have felt good for him all day long, his intention. Good to tell the doctors in the lunchroom that he was sorry, he couldn't have a drink after work, he was picking up the children. Good father that he was.

And then what? He'd get into his car, and instead of turning left, he'd turn right? Just like that and fast, probably? He would drive fast, away from where they were standing, two children who cared more about him than anyone else in the world ever would. Two of them dressed in matching outfits, not talking, Margaret had noticed—they didn't talk while they were waiting, just kept silent watch, and meanwhile he would be pressing the pedal to the metal and turning up the radio as he drove in the opposite direction. *"Volare,"* he would be singing, as the two children were finally led back into the house. *"Cantare, oh oh oh oh."*

Did he know? Did he have a clue? Maybe not, but didn't that constitute evil too?

Sim Richardson pointed out that he was one of those charmers. "Everyone loves him," he told Margaret.

"Not me," she'd answered, and Sim had smiled.

"*I see, said the blind man,*" he had intoned, in his preacher's voice.

But did he? Did he see what she saw? He was there that day to fix the cellar door. The children had gone out to play with the neighbors the other day, a Sunday, and somehow the back door had gotten locked and Lora had snatched a rare nap, and hadn't heard the doorbell. Josie had panicked and thought that maybe she was dead inside, and gone to the neighbor's father, a big strong man, and begged him to break down the cellar door. And then Lora had come down in her bathrobe, mortified, and had to call Sim in to fix it.

Not a small job either, but did he see the pit, the abyss, that the children were hanging over by a thread? Although she was thinking that maybe the worst was behind them. He hadn't called for a while now. Lora told Margaret that even if he did call with one of his pretenses of coming, they wouldn't tell the children.

"If he comes, we can get them," she said.

He won't come, Margaret didn't bother to answer.

Josie couldn't have said afterward when it had stopped. Her desperate calls to the Medical Dental Bureau. Her waking from bad dreams to a wet bed. It finally just happened that no one in the house was talking about him anymore. He had stopped calling, dangling his counterfeit promises that still glittered like gold before her eyes. His voice, though sounding brass by now to the world at large, that was still music to her ears.

"Children adapt," the grown-ups agreed, and the children did. They were happy. Did well in school. Played on all the teams. Had friends. Other fathers stepped in when called for. Lora became a Little League coach, called Willie by his last name, "Brier," like the fathers did. Their uncles came to visit from out of town, and their grandparents gradually occupied the house. Got rid of the relics—the pipe music box, his initials on the bedspread. The last of his clothes went to Sim Richardson.

They had moved on—except some nights, when Josie found herself alone in one of the rooms with the curtains drawn, and she could slip behind and gaze into the icy windows, frosted with a glaze that reflected back her eyes—his eyes.

"Come back," she would pray to him then, but silently, so no one ever knew. Except for him—he would know, she was still thinking, hoping. Maybe. He hadn't forgotten. She could see him, almost, his eyes, like hers. His eyebrows, her eyebrows.

"Come back," she would whisper, and sometimes it almost felt then like he had. Some nights, she could almost see him gazing, seriously, fully, no withholding, back at her, love in his eyes.

HARRIET AND ELIZABETH

Margaret looked over at Josie, who was standing in the doorway. Big now, twelve, or was it thirteen? Tall for her age, maybe fully grown, but still with that skinny look. Just on the verge. She'd recently started wearing little cotton bras, and begged Margaret not to hang them out on the line, where the boys could see them. But Margaret knew that.

Knew a lot, but not everything, it turned out. Or maybe knew, but found herself forgetting. Mostly in private, mostly something she could cover, to herself, in her mind, like when she woke up the other day and found herself looking around her room—or at least the room that they'd called hers, for five or six years now—and had to take some time to put together where she was. Gazing at the pictures on her battered bureau—her sons, she knew that, but what about the bureau? The bedspread, and whose rooftop was that, out her window? Nice slates, but a lot of them broken. Who lived there?

But luckily there was no one there to ask, and she'd pulled herself back from whatever brink that was before she put on her white uniform—if she'd seen that hanging there, if her closet had been open, of course she'd have known right off, but it wouldn't be. Open. Her closet door. She wasn't careless that way, or any way. She took great care.

Although she was caught out the other day, in all the to-do around getting Josie ready for her first dancing class, with boys. Margaret knew the boys—most of them came up to Josie's chin, she and Lora had had a secret laugh about it, but Josie was excited, and Margaret was part of it, undoing her braids, fixing her hair back into a nice ponytail, when Lora came in with the nylon stockings, which Josie had begged to wear, instead of her white anklets.

Margaret had looked up and without thinking had offered to roll Josie's nylons for her. "I can do them up really smooth," she'd said.

Both Lora and Josie had turned to her, surprised—Josie almost offended. Nobody rolled their stockings anymore, Margaret was informed.

And of course she knew that. Knew that even Lora had never rolled her stockings. That it had been thirty years since girls whose parents could afford those garments with the little click garters had rolled their stockings.

But just at that moment, when she'd seen Josie opening the package of her first pair of nylons, seen them coming out of the cellophane, still untouched and lightly shaded, she'd been swept back to her own early dancing days, and the way she and her sisters used to roll their stockings.

With such skill and dexterity that they never bagged, never fell down. And the time it took, to make sure their stockings, much thicker than these, the cheapest money could buy, were so tight and smooth that they looked almost like silk. Which she'd believed, now that she thought about it, would get her somewhere in this world. That that combination of skill and care would be noticed, somehow, by someone, and with that person's help, she would become a teacher, or an assistant in a flower shop. Work commensurate with the way she rolled her stockings.

Well, that hadn't come to pass, but it was what Margaret had been thinking about, what had overcome her that day when she offered to roll Josie's stockings. Not that she could explain that to them—all she could do was look like a crazy old woman who still thought that in 1963, white girls in big houses still rolled their stockings.

And then the next week, she had burned a pie. For the

first time in her entire life. And then slept through break-fast, and Lora had called the doctor, who listened to her heart and asked her if she was thinking of retiring.

Which was why, in a week or so, her son, Boyd, would be coming to take her home—though it wasn't to her home, it was to his home. With a wife who didn't want her.

On an Army base, in western Pennsylvania, so that part was good. Not too far from where she'd been born, where her boys had been born, although she wasn't sure if the other two were around there these days. The old-est, Charles, was the kind of minister who traveled a cir-cuit and didn't have much of a home, or maybe even a wife anymore—she hadn't heard from him for a while. And James was out of the picture ever since he married a white girl.

Unless she'd already left him, being that kind of woman, the kind of white woman who would marry a Black man. Not to mention her son being the kind of Black man who would marry a cheap woman because she was white, blinded to the truth that she was beneath him. Cheap and mean and always treating him badly. From the start, Margaret had seen it, she cheated and drank, but he loved her, because she was white. Margaret hated that.

"Is she pretty?" Josie had asked her once.

Margaret admitted she was, "in a cheap way," and Josie imagined her looking like one of her friends' mothers who wore a see-through nightgown most of the day, and was fat, with her hair dyed black.

But Margaret said James's wife was skinny, and her hair was dyed blond, not black.

"Are you sad?" Josie was asking her, from the doorway. Margaret had gotten a phone call that morning from one of her sons, with the news that her husband—ex-husband—had died, and Lora had given her the rest of the day off. She'd gone up to the third floor and taken off her shoes. They still hurt, despite the holes she'd cut out for her toes.

How long had it been? she was trying to remember. She hadn't loved him for years, at least not enough to live with him anymore, or send him money.

But it wasn't as if they hadn't had their time. He was father to her last son, Boyd, the best one, the tall one, and there'd been those days—nights—when he'd made her happy, like no man ever had. When her hair was long and black and hanging down her back, and he called her Maggie. Never Margaret.

"Maggie girl," even though she had the two other boys by then, Charles and James. That was in McKeesport, up a steep hill that froze all winter and the buses couldn't get up, didn't bother. But the boys loved it—would scavenge some plywood and slide down. And then one Christmas, he, her husband in deed if not in word, had come home with a real sled.

A Flexible Flyer. Boyd was a baby, but Charles and James were ecstatic. "Just be careful at the bottom!" she'd called after them. It was a busy street, dangerous.

"Turn!" her husband had taught them. Showed them how the Flexible Flyer, a little bit beaten-up but still working, could turn to the side, so as not to careen into a streetcar. And that was what she'd been thinking about—not his drinking, not his betrayal. That Christmas and him and the boys, when Josie had appeared in the doorway.

"You're not sad, are you?"

What could she say? That he had been beautiful to her? That he was Boyd's father, and tall and strong? A real workingman, only it was hard for Black men to get real work. That she had hoped, believed, for a while that maybe he could find work that would keep him, that would be worth his brains and strength, his life, and that then maybe they would stay together.

"'Cause you were divorced"—Margaret knew what Josie was saying. She wanted her to say that she wasn't sad, since she shouldn't be sad, being divorced. That if you're divorced, when he dies, you shouldn't have to come upstairs to the top of the house, in the middle of the day, and lie on your bed and wish you'd seen him one more time.

That you'd give anything to see him again.

"Margaret's just tired," she said to Josie. She didn't mention the "Maggie girl" part, though she almost could have. Josie was on the brink of understanding. Reading grown-up books from Lora's bookshelf. Going to dancing class in nylons.

She asked if Margaret wanted some tea or a ginger ale, but Margaret said no, and closed her eyes, though she was touched. She'd been the one bringing tea and ginger ale to Josie, as she lay in bed all those years ago, with the kind of sickness that had no name. Lovesickness. Loss.

That was the past too, though. Just like the stockings she'd rolled, the future that had turned out not to be there for her after all. The other day, she overheard the baby, Timmy—but he was six now, almost seven. Still her baby, though. He still loved her.

But she heard him ask Josie, "Is Uncle Leonard Daddy?"

And she had frozen, but to her relief, Josie had laughed. "No one told him!" she'd said, amazed, turning to Margaret. She explained that they'd had a father, like everyone else, but didn't anymore. It turned out they didn't need one. They had their uncles, their grandfather, Lora. The best mother in the world instead, Josie told Timmy, in the most matter-of-fact way.

And Margaret realized then how profoundly they'd moved on. Nobody here, not even Lora, would be taking to their rooms now if their former father, as Josie styled him, died. He was so absent, so gone, that Timmy, at six years old, had never even heard his name, which must not have been spoken at any time he could remember in this house.

All those years. All that pain and loss, and who could count the cost, for Josie, and Willie too? He used to cry nights for his father when he was four, but now he was "Brier," on the ball field. "Good arm, Brier," other boys' fathers would shout to him, and Margaret took pride for her part in that. She'd thrown the ball to him in the backyard, with her strong arm, making up for no father, and then too brought him up on the stories of her own boys, especially Boyd, who'd gone into the military and become a boxing champ. One of the uncles had gotten Willie some boxing gloves and satin shorts for his birthday, and she had shown him how to hold his hands up, and someone had taken a picture of her, with him, his fists raised. He was skinny, and she towered above him, in her white uniform, always neat, always pressed, smile on her face.

Josie crept in and sat on the edge of Margaret's bed. She'd never seen her that way before, lying there, eyes closed. It didn't seem like Margaret. But it was—there were her shoes beside the bed, unmistakable, like no one's shoes.

White leather, but with the sides cut out around her toes, which were always "aching," she said. An old-fashioned word. No one said "ache" anymore.

Margaret said "commode" too, for bathroom. Toilet. And Margaret had actually thought she, Josie, would roll her stockings. Like someone from the olden days, from the backwoods somewhere.

She knew Margaret was leaving, but realized now that she'd always assumed it would be with a *"band of angels,"* in the *"sweet chariot"* she used to sing to them about, to send them off to sleep. With her low, soft voice, and Josie had seen that chariot, though in her mind it was soft, made of bulrushes, like Moses's basket. The truth was she didn't quite know what a real chariot was anyway.

"Coming for to carry me home," Margaret used to sing, and Josie had just assumed that would be how it went, how she would go, but now it wouldn't be a chariot after all. It would be Boyd's car.

And the *"band of angels"*—they weren't coming now, but would they, someday? When Margaret died? Maybe that's what Margaret had meant all along.

They had to come, after all that singing. All that believing. At least come for Margaret—it seemed only fair. Josie didn't think anyone in her family believed, or thought much about it. Bands of angels or sweet chariots. Maybe because this side of Jordan was good enough for them.

Josie remembered the stories Margaret used to tell her some nights, when she was still up after Willie had gone to sleep. About Harriet and Elizabeth, two little girls Margaret had cared for, years ago. She had loved them—both so good, though only Elizabeth was beautiful. With long hair—

"Dark or light?" Josie would ask. Hers was dark.

"Dark," Margaret would say, and Josie knew just who she looked like, the beautiful girl next door, with her long hair, plaid kilts, and knee socks. But Josie could never quite see Harriet, who was just as good, "but homely," said Margaret. She drew it out, the old-fashioned word, in her old-fashioned way. "Hoome-ly."

"Like who?" Josie would ask her, but she never could say. Just that "she had a short lip," which was beyond Josie's capability of picturing. She preferred the beautiful Elizabeth anyway, until the part where Elizabeth, now grown up and married, with two little daughters of her own, was sleeping one calm winter's night, and her house caught fire and they were all burned up in their beds.

Now, looking at Margaret, lying there on the sagging mattress, in a room with all the cast-off furniture that none of them wanted, Josie wondered if the story was true. She'd once asked Margaret where they'd lived and she'd said New Castle, but another time she'd said East Palestine—could Margaret have made Harriet and Elizabeth up?

But then why make up the truly horrible death for Elizabeth for no reason? Since she'd been just as nice as Harriet.

Or was it for all the reasons? Margaret's lifetime of old furniture on people's third floors? What had it been like for Margaret, to sing her sweet chariot song and tiptoe out of Josie's lovely room with wallpaper and a nice thick rug, up the back stairs with the old worn carpeting, to her own inferior quarters, despite her superior talents? The care she took, her cleaning, her ironing, the way she starched Josie's grandfather's shirts "just right," and her pies, "the best in town"? But wasn't she paid the same thirty dollars as the maid next door, who put marshmallows on canned sweet potatoes on Friday nights and called it good?

Was that why Elizabeth burned up in her bed? And what could be done now to save her, or, really, to save Margaret? Maybe there would be a chariot, or even God himself to say, *Well done, Margaret. You did the best you could. Come over.*

To what, though? Josie tried to imagine what would make Margaret truly happy. What could pay her back for a lifetime of injustice, hard work? Bands of singing angels? Peace and tranquility? Margaret had once told her that when she was Josie's age, or maybe a little older, she'd wanted to go to teachers' college, or even nursing school. Well, that hadn't happened.

Josie got up and tiptoed out. She hoped when Margaret's son came, he would wear his uniform. The boys were excited about that. She'd overheard her grandmother interviewing a new woman, who would move upstairs to Margaret's room, when she left.

It would be hard to say goodbye. She didn't want to be there when she left, but Margaret had promised that Boyd would bring her back to visit. Josie hoped so. If not, there still might be *"God's golden shore,"* as another of Margaret's songs put it. Josie had pictured that, with late afternoon sunshine. Maybe she would get there too, and even Harriet and Elizabeth, and Margaret would walk among them all, take care of them, but wouldn't sleep in their houses.

One thing Josie was sure of—on the other side of Jordan, Margaret would have a house of her own.

— VIII —

THE L-SHAPED ROOM

When Josie picked up *Wuthering Heights* again, thirty years after first reading, she felt as if she'd swum unawares into a riptide, the kind they say will drop you back on the shore if you don't panic and fight it—in this case, the shore being her girlhood bedroom. Though she'd started rereading the book in a house edging on the Pacific, with three half-grown children to her name, when she next looked up she had landed in the bedroom with ballerinas on the wallpaper and the snow piled high all around. Her mother, grandparents, and brothers were asleep in the bedrooms around her, and she was fourteen again, ranging wild with Cathy Earnshaw across the moors. There was much there that she couldn't understand then. Marriage and revenge marriage—she herself would have been happy to marry Edgar, live at the Grange and leave it at that. As for Cathy and Heathcliff, their wild and tragic attraction and destruction left a fourteen-year-old American girl rereading their words with no real clue of what they were talking about.

But the ghosts at the windows—that was something she knew. All those years of her own searching, her eyes in the icy panes, reflected, refracted back. Her eyebrows, her eyes. Like his, which was where she sought him, where she saw him, but by fourteen that was over. Then, when she went to the icy window late at night, she wasn't looking for her father anymore. She was looking for Heathcliff. Holden Caulfield. L. B. Turner, the older boy next door who'd gone away to college and barely knew her name, which left her safe in her schoolgirl bed.

In that state of pure green, untouched still in Artemis's woods, but less inclined, month by month, to turn the dogs on a handsome young hunter who might venture in. She was tall for her age, and a good runner, but already no Hippolyta. On the contrary, she liked the boys she knew, though they were small and skinny and good only for winning twist contests at the boy-girl parties she had been starting to attend.

That summer, she was invited to spend the night with a school friend, who lived way out in the country, in a poor, broken-down part of the world with little pink houses, wood on cinder block, the kind of people, she had heard, who went to Baptist meetings and nudist camps in West Virginia in the summer.

"What a nice house," said Lora, unconvincingly, as she drove Josie up the rutted dirt driveway, past a few old cars up on blocks in the front yard. There was an abandoned bicycle on the ground—no kickstands out here—but there were no sidewalks to ride on anyway, so who cared?

"The sticks," people called it. No longer the country. Josie's grandparents used to drive her out here to buy corn when she was little, but now they had to go farther. Ever since these houses had gone up, near the school. Which had brought in a new demographic—blue collar instead of the farmers, whom Lora had liked better. Liked their practical smarts, and their humor. "The cows don't hold with daylight savings, and neither do we." "The rooster does the crowing, but the hens deliver the goods."

It was to teach the farm kids that Lora took the job out at that country school—the smart ones who stayed late for the school newspaper and basketball. Played the trumpet— the boys—and piano—the girls—and read all the books she gave them. *David Copperfield. The Scarlet Letter.* Emerson's essays. Walden Pond. Lora's American dream, these kids were.

The new people's kids were less of a sure thing. Their fathers worked at the mills or wrecking yards, and their children didn't have the grounding of the farm kids. Some yes, some no. More likely to be going into the military than to Kent or Oberlin.

"Have fun," said Lora, and Josie had a pang as her mother drove away, leaving her among this slightly alien tribe of people. But her friend came running out, her blond ponytail bouncing, and she and Josie went into the kitchen. The parents weren't at home, but there were some cute cousins, high school girls who'd brought over a transistor radio, and they sat at the table, drinking lemonade and fiddling with the dial. You could sometimes get Pittsburgh, and when they finally did, there was Bobby Vinton, singing "Blue on blue, heartache on heartache"—which they all joined, shouting it out, laughing together.

Josie's friend's brother came into the kitchen. "What's going on?"

He was fifteen or so, one of the older boys Josie had only glimpsed from a distance. She knew he was one of those good students who played basketball, so was someone Lora liked. But he was cooler than the farm boys, with blond hair combed back, and a girlfriend who came to school in tight skirts and a bouffant hairdo. Makeup. Definitely not one of Lora's nice, scrubbed, college-bound girls.

Josie felt her face turn red when he said hi to her, though it wasn't the hi, it was the way he looked at her, just fast, in passing, the way people did. But then he stopped and looked again, looked twice. That hadn't happened before. She'd looked away quickly—that hadn't happened before either.

And then, later, when the cousins left and she and his sister were out in the yard tossing a ball, he came out and started talking to her, teasing, joking around. He had on jeans and a white T-shirt—the kind you weren't allowed to wear to school—with a pack of cigarettes in his back pocket. None of the boys she knew dressed remotely like that. They wore . . . she didn't know what they wore. Children's clothes. Shirts. Pants. Shorts. Whatever their parents gave them.

There was a clothesline across the small yard, with sheets and towels hanging out to dry, and he walked around, behind the sheets, hidden from the kitchen window, and called to her, "Tug-of-war." He pulled a towel from the line and threw her an end, which she caught, but then, before she knew what was happening, he pulled her straight to him and kissed her on the lips.

She was stunned. She'd kissed boys before—Spin the Bottle, card games, but this was something different.

She didn't remember the rest of the visit. She barely slept that night, in his sister's little bedroom. She kept replaying that kiss, the way he'd taken her by surprise, by ambush, pulling her to him like that. Tossing her the towel—"Tug-of-war!"—after looking at her twice, and then kissing her like someone in the movies. A tug-of-war that had pulled her to the other side of a divide.

She put on her shorts in the morning—they were too short, she realized, what kids wore. She would ask Lora to get her some Bermudas, and maybe get her hair cut. Ponytails were for kids. His sister asked if she wanted to play jacks, but she didn't. She wanted to play tug-of-war.

Although she was relieved not to see him again that morning. She'd heard his mother yelling at him earlier, and then a door slam. Breakfast was "hotcakes," as they said, which in her house was usually a festive occasion, but here was mostly silent. Was that how these people were, or was it her fault? But what had she done? She hadn't done anything—or had she?

Was it her fault, what had happened? Did they know? Blame her? She was surprised, but also relieved, when her friend's mother said she would drive her home, right after breakfast. The plan had been for them to take her later, but the mother said she had to go into town now and couldn't go twice. Josie's friend wanted to come too, but her mother wouldn't let her. Left her to do the dishes—a real punishment, Josie felt, so they must be mad at her too.

Josie and the mother got into the car and sat mostly in silence. The mother was wearing old shorts, and a sleeveless cotton shirt, and her arms were fat. Josie looked out the window. Did she really have something to do, or did she just want to get rid of her? They'd seemed glad to see her at first, treated her like an honored guest.

Had her friend told, about the kiss? Did they blame her? Were they right? Had it been her fault?

They pulled into her drive, and the mother turned to her and asked if she'd had a good time. Josie said, yes, thank you, and the mother seemed like she wanted to say something else, but she didn't, just shrugged, and Josie jumped out of the car and ran into the house. Timmy was still at the breakfast table, and her grandmother was making French toast, but Josie went straight upstairs. She threw down her little overnight bag with her nightgown and toothbrush, which she'd forgotten to bring when she went into the bathroom the night before, and then hadn't wanted to risk going back for, possibly bumping into anyone—him—in the hall.

Now she brushed her teeth, and looked in the mirror. Still okay, she thought. Her eyes, her nose, nothing changed, nothing marking. She hopped on her bike and pedaled as fast as she could over to her friend Suzie's. They got a towel from the bathroom and went outside, behind the garage, where no one could see them.

She threw Suzie the towel, yelled, "Tug-of-war," and then reeled her in, just like he had, and kissed her hard. Just like he had kissed her, only the feeling with Suzie wasn't there, and they both burst out laughing. They were still skinny, still had their hair in ponytails, and had only just stopped wearing their Cleveland Indian T-shirts. Prized possessions that they'd gotten a few years ago, when Suzie's father had taken them to a baseball game in Cleveland.

"What do you want to do?" asked Suzie, but Josie wasn't sure. Go for a bike ride? See if her neighbors were playing Capture the Flag?

But was that something she still did? Finally, they rode over to a friend's house with older sisters and movie magazines. One of the sisters took Josie into the bathroom and plucked her thick eyebrows. When she came home, Lora had a fit.

"My God! " she cried. "What happened?"

"Terry's sister—"

Lora was furious, and ready to call the mother, call the police, "This is outrageous!" But Josie started to cry, and then couldn't stop, kept crying, until Lora hugged her and took her upstairs, into the bathroom with the good mirror, and penciled her eyebrows back in.

"This isn't who you are," Lora told her, "those plucked eyebrows," and Josie nodded, willing to believe her, because she had no idea who she was. A day ago she'd been Josie Brier, a girl with a mother and two brothers, who loved books and ran fast and wished she had a bulldog. She didn't tell Lora that she was also now a girl a boy had looked at twice and then kissed. Went to some trouble to kiss, devised a way. And that she wasn't sure after that who she was. Maybe even a girl with plucked eyebrows.

Years later, she would read in Rilke, "*There are no classes in life for beginners, always what is hardest is demanded of you right away*," and she knew it was true. Remembered it was true.

A few months after that, she got her hair cut short and went to a party and won a dance contest—a record, the Chiffons, singing "He's so Fine." Catherine, who was working for them then, had taught her how to dance, with small steps. The twist was over, and other kids her age were doing the monkey, but Catherine had showed her another way. Cool and contained, like Catherine herself, who was beautiful and worked there days, but, unlike Margaret, couldn't live upstairs. She had two daughters, Marilyn and Carolyn, who were in high school and going to college, and a husband named Coalman, which caused her no end of trouble, said Catherine.

"Not the man," said Catherine, "but the name." Because there was a faith healer called Kathryn Kuhlman, who came through town every year, and filled the Stambaugh Auditorium with true believers who wanted her touch. Cripples who would throw away their crutches, the blind who would see the light, all well and good, but people got *Kuhlman* mixed up with *Coalman*, and would stop Catherine in the street, begging her to cure them.

"And I explain, but they still want me to touch their diseases, and believe me, I'm not the nursing type." She shook her head. "People!"

"Why can't they get it straight?" said Catherine. Like the other day, someone said they'd heard she was working at Dr. Brier's house, when it hadn't been his house for all these years.

"I told them I was working for Mrs. Brier, not him!"— but Josie had been stopped by the name and didn't hear that part. It was funny—she was mostly on guard, but every once in a while, something would hit her, out of the blue. When she wasn't expecting it, when the drawbridge was down. Then her face would get hot, her ears start burning.

"Dr. Brier." "Your father"—it used to be worse, though. Used to happen just at the mention of the word "father," mostly at school. In books when they were learning to read—"Dick," "Jane," "Mother," "Father." Just the word would pin her to the page, underneath all the eyes in the classroom that she feared were turned on her. The one girl in the class without one. "Father."

But that didn't happen anymore. Nor did the specific words "your father" freeze her like they used to. As in, "*Your father loves you very much,*" half whispered by some dastardly parent, who would occasionally corner her at a children's party. Speaking low, like a drug pusher, singling her out, what she most hated and dreaded, ruining the tail she was pinning on the donkey, a child among children. And she knew them even then for what they were—ill-meaning enemies of hers and Lora's, who had ripped her from the cozy group to stand her alone on the sidelines, to whisper demonically in her small ear that the man who had left her crawling on the shore, stranded in the street, missed her terribly and sent his love.

Josie learned to spot them—they shared an approach. A quick glance from side to side to make sure no one who could stop them was looking, one of Lora's friends—and eventually to evade them. She would take the hand of one of her friends, or pretend not to see them if they beckoned, which worked until life carried her along. The parties she attended no longer had parents standing in the shadows.

And then too, it had been a long time since she'd even seen him. First months, and then a year. Two years. Three, maybe—she was no longer counting. She brought home Peter, Paul and Mary from another party, and forgot she'd ever had a father as she sat replaying "Blowin' in the Wind."

How many roads did a man really have to walk down? she wondered. She'd never thought about it before. She looked at the album cover—Mary's long straight hair, Peter and Paul's beards, and then turned it over and read the notes on the back. The next week, she took three dollars to Record Rendezvous, and asked for a Bob Dylan album.

"Dye-lan," she said. She hadn't heard his name spoken yet.

Mr. Crouse smiled. "Dillon," he told her, and pulled out *The Times They Are A-Changin'*.

The voice was harsh and sounded like a bum's, but pretty soon she liked it, then loved it. Because Dylan was right, the times were changing. When he sang, *"Come mothers and fathers, throughout the land, and don't criticize what you can't understand,"* she sang right along with him, at the top of her lungs. The word "father" didn't stop her there.

Like Bob Dylan, she was beyond his command.

The next year, she was in ninth grade, and a senior boy started coming around. She'd heard that he'd been kicked out of boarding school for having a girl in his room, which gave him cachet before she'd even met him.

It wasn't as if he were the best-looking boy she knew. He was short and wore the same shirt over and over—one of those blue-and-red-striped rugby things—but when he asked her out to the movies, it was a French film called *Band of Outsiders*, and right then she changed her idea of the girl she wanted to be. Not smiling up at some Hollywood leading man, but riding in an old sports car, reading a book. Dancing with two men with a hat on her head in some dingy café. And when the movie ended, she felt like a different person from when she'd gone in, and afterward, the boy kissed her ear in a way that confirmed that everything had changed.

She came home twice after that in wrinkled woolen skirts that resulted in a curfew. Which she was prepared to break, and gave transgressive thanks that there was no father in the house, only an old grandfather who would be easier to slip past.

Because she had no "No" for this boy, no defenses against what he was offering. She was an A student, passionate even about her French, but there was no French anymore, no *Mill on the Floss*, no practicing dances, even, with Bennie Mae, who had replaced Catherine in the kitchen these days. She barely spoke at the dinner table anymore, and never had dessert. Just went up to her room, hoping the phone would ring. Praying, even, that he would call her that night.

Lora was alarmed. She'd never had to worry about Josie before, but she'd seen the wrinkled skirts, and even the marks on her neck, which no longer appeared after Lora had started questioning her. But were there marks that she couldn't see? Josie started locking the door when she took a bath, and weren't the skirts that weren't wrinkled telling a tale of their own? A worse tale?

Lora wasn't sure what to do—should she order the boy out of the yard when he came over in the afternoon? He was no longer asking Josie out on proper dates, which she could have forbidden, but maybe they were meeting at parties? Should she stop Josie from going out at all?

Did that work? She thought of her own story—hadn't she been forbidden from marrying Martin Brier? And of course her parents had been right, but what was that, up against the kind of surprise raid that batters a girl's walls and breaks down her gates? Or just catches her, walking through the wildflowers, unawares.

Lora knew that passion, only too well, before and after, both in haste and at leisure, and she'd recognized it once when the boy's name had escaped her daughter's lips when they'd turned into their driveway after school one day, and there, to their mutual surprise, was his car.

Josie had whispered his name out loud. Hadn't been able to stop herself. Lora was frightened, not sure where to turn. Her brothers? Ask one of them to drive down from Cleveland and tell this boy, man-to-man, to get lost and never come back? Or even her ex-husband, Josie's father, whose job it should have been.

Although going to any of them would reveal them both— her as incompetent, unable to secure her own borders, with a daughter who might not be as nice as she looked. That was really what was stopping her—betraying Josie. Pulling back the curtain on her young life.

And would they think she was a slut, a tramp? Wasn't

that the way they would take it, the men? Blaming Josie, when what she needed was protection?

Lora barely slept those nights. A few days later, at breakfast, she looked at Josie's hand and noticed her little ring was gone. She always wore it—it had been Lora's grandmother's, a very pretty small gold ring with a little diamond set delicately in the middle.

Lora frowned—Josie saw her, saw where her eyes had been, and quickly put her hand on her lap, under the table, out of sight. She had given the ring to the boy—he had asked for it, and she had taken it to mean that he liked her, maybe loved her, though she heard from some girls at school that he'd done it on a dare. He had another girl's ring too, they told her. It was a joke to him. Josie's face got hot just thinking about it.

She was prepared to lie to Lora, to tell her that she had lost the ring, was looking for it, would get it back, had left it at a friend's house. But Lora didn't ask, which Josie feared meant that she knew.

When Josie read *War and Peace* five years later, she knew what Tolstoy meant when he talked about luck and accidents driving one's fate. She thought back, to when she had no control over her own actions. She didn't even think about them, was more a prisoner just waiting for him to call or come by and free her temporarily, which he mostly didn't.

Josie had heard that he had another girlfriend besides her—he'd even mentioned her himself, couldn't resist talking about her. She was eighteen, so older, cooler, a senior in the high school across town, and Josie had heard from her friends that she was "cute," with short black hair, a pixie cut. Once when he and Josie had slipped down to the basement to "play ping-pong," he showed her how he could put his arms around her and kiss her while bouncing the ping-pong ball behind her back. He said it was the other girl's mother who'd taught him that trick. Told him that's what she and her boyfriend used to do, when she was young.

So, a cool mother, as opposed to Lora, whom Josie had caught recently telling him she wasn't home when he finally called. She'd burst into tears and run to her room, slammed the door for the first time in her life. Or what about her grandfather, who had actually come down to the basement when they were, thank goodness, in fact playing ping-pong and ordered her up to dinner? At four o'clock in the afternoon.

Josie had wanted to scream at her grandfather, and to tell the boy that her grandfather was just a stupid old man with no authority over her, none at all, but the boy had left too quickly, fled, really, before she had a chance to explain. So even though he'd told her not to call him, she decided to risk it that night, just to let him know that she didn't care anything at all about her grandfather. That she'd rather he lie down and die than to ever interfere in her life again. Their lives.

But when, heart pounding, hand shaking, she finally dialed his number, his mother answered the phone and said he wasn't home, though it was a school night, and then he didn't call her back.

Where was he? At the other girl's house? On a school night? But that was the thing—she, the other girl, had a cool mother, so there it was. Instead of coming to see her, he was there, where the mother was glad to see him and even charm him with stories about her own misbehavior. Offering fun and laughs instead of the stone-cold silence that met him at her door.

One night, not long after, he actually asked her out properly, to a movie, and Lora, informed that they were going with a group of friends—a lie—had said a reluctant okay. It was a double feature, Josie told her, *Hud* and *The L-Shaped Room*, at the art house down by the college.

Only they didn't go to the movies, but instead spent those few hours in his car, parked out on the edge of things. Then he said he had to go by his house, to "get something." She didn't dare wonder what.

He'd left her in the car and run inside, and while she was waiting, his father had come out and walked over. She was embarrassed already, just to be sitting out there alone, in that car that night. Did his father know what they'd been up to? Right there, in the car, instead of watching an art-house movie?

He smiled at her, and she wasn't sure what that smile meant, if it was the straightforward approval she was used to, the way other people's fathers smiled at her, the A student, their daughters' nice friend. Was this tinged with something else? Knowing?

Because she wasn't the A student in that car that night, or even nice. All she was, was a fool for this man's son, and all that mattered was his soft voice in her ear. His striped shirts and long blond hair that he tossed back. His light green eyes.

She was fifteen. She knew it was wrong, she was wrong, subject to any disapproval this man might throw at her, or, worse, at her mother, whom he might now find permissive, incapable of protecting a daughter. But right then, none of what she usually lived for mattered to Josie. What mattered was that she was there, this night, with the only thing in life she cared about, and that soon he would come out of the house, and sit beside her again. Drive her wherever he wanted her to go. A party, he'd said, just outside of town.

"How was the movie?" his father asked, with his unsettling smile.

Josie took a breath. At least he wasn't part of Lora's immediate social world, though everyone knew him. But he definitely wasn't one of the close-knit group of her friends' fathers—maybe his business was slightly shady, or his wife was from somewhere else, was someone nobody knew. Anyway, she'd never seen them out anywhere with anyone else that she knew. They had an older daughter who was severely retarded. Very sad. In a home somewhere.

"It was, uh, good."

"What did you see?"

She'd forgotten it was a double feature.

"*The L-Shaped Room*," she said, and he'd smiled. Again, a smile she wasn't used to.

"You should have seen *Hud*," he said. "I heard it was better."

He walked back to the house and caught his son coming out, on the front porch. She could see them, arguing, though she couldn't hear. Still, the father was pointing his finger at his son, and talking angrily into his ear.

His son got back in the car. "You said *The L-Shaped Room*, right?"

"Yeah."

"I told him we'd seen *Hud*."

"Oh no—"

She was mortified, but he just laughed. Though instead of turning right, out of town, toward the party, he turned left, down her street. "Change of plans."

She nodded. He pulled into her drive. Didn't try to kiss her.

" 'Bye," he said.

She stumbled out of the car, in tears of shame and grief. How could she ever face his father?

Though it turned out she didn't have to. She never saw him again.

That was the end of his son too. They had never used the word "love" between them. She barely even knew him, at least by any regular measures. Didn't know what kind of ice cream he liked, what books he read, or probably didn't read, because he mostly cut school, people told her. But what did he do, then, all day? She had no idea, he had never mentioned anything about his life—but this she only realized afterward. When she was trying to remember what they'd talked about, and ended up concluding that they'd hardly talked at all.

But that wasn't to say that she didn't love him. That night, after he dropped her off, she heard that he'd gone on to the party without her, and the other girl was there, the one who was older, eighteen. A few months later, she got a breathless call from a friend who'd seen the girl in the bathroom at school, rolling up her skirt over what looked like a fat round stomach. And soon after that, the girl disappeared from school, and rumor had it that she'd been sent to a home for unwed mothers in Kentucky, where you had your baby in a dark room with no names.

Why name it, since it would be whisked straight out for adoption, even before you came to, and you would never see it again?

It was winter when Josie heard all this. She grabbed her skates and walked down to the park, and slipped out onto the pond. It was freezing, but it hadn't snowed for a while, and the old man in charge had swept the ice for a change, so it was fairly smooth. No one else was out—too cold, too late, getting dark. Perfect.

She skated fast all the way down to the edge of the creek, and then back. This was her then, still a girl, a skater on a cold winter's day. Not an unwed mother in some place of disgrace, hidden away and yet in full sight, since everyone knew. Even her, the would-be rival who had escaped unharmed.

What had saved her? Not her, not him. He hadn't pushed

her that far, but he could have, and she would have been helpless to stop him.

So what was it? She paged back through the months, and came to *The L-Shaped Room*, and his father, standing there on the porch, pointing his finger, clearly angry about something—about her? Had he taken pity on a fatherless girl sitting alone in the car that night, waiting, impassioned, on the edge of her seat? Telling him childish lies about what movie his son hadn't taken her to that night?

And pity, too, for Lora and her brave attempts to raise her family alone? And maybe it encompassed her old grandfather as well, who was doing his best to stand in for a proper father who could have chased the boy off. Even just the shadow of a man in the window.

Maybe that father, on that porch, was standing in for that absence that night. Extending the protection of the fathers to her after all.

But as for the other girl, her unprotected doppelgänger, she never heard what happened to her, or the baby. Occasionally she found herself doing the math—*He or she would be twenty now, incredible*, and so on.

But did the mother even finish high school? She didn't think she'd shown up back in town. Maybe she started another life somewhere else. Maybe she'd put her pleated skirts back on and her knee socks and gone to some high school nearby, disguised as just another cute girl. Maybe from there she went to college, married or didn't marry, became a teacher or nurse or secretary.

Or maybe she stayed the path and became a pole dancer in Las Vegas, which was just heating up in those days. A stripper, a high-end prostitute. Maybe one of the girls in the home for unwed mothers in Kentucky showed her the way.

That spring, Josie found herself buying tiny books with sweet little round-faced children, where "Love" was bouquets of flowers and cute visits to ice-cream parlors, as opposed to breathless grapplings in backseats, and lies to people's fathers. She went to see the *Mary Poppins* film five times, becoming for those hours the little girl with a navy-blue hat with streamers, like the one that Lora had bought her years ago when Best & Co. came to town, and that she'd hated with passion when forced to wear it.

And there was a new French teacher at school, a shy young man from Lebanon who actually spoke French, as opposed to the farm woman he'd replaced, and before long, Josie was reading *Le Petit Prince*, and finding that life didn't have to be desperate to be promising, didn't have to send her rushing to the window—*Let it be him*—every time a car seemed to stop.

Au contraire, as she learned to say. French was calm, French was cold, French was sophisticated, and French was her future. She would go to France one day, and walk down the Champs-Élysées with two Russian wolfhounds, wearing a Piaget watch like the ones in the *New York Times*, to which Lora had recently subscribed. A few months later, she added to the picture a mini–fur coat, like the one George Harrison's girlfriend was photographed wearing, because the Beatles had broken by then.

And to the dream of cool France was added swinging London.

"Which one would you marry?" she and her friends asked each other.

Paul was easy—of course they'd marry Paul, or George, if Paul didn't ask them. John was out, since he was already married, but, "Would you marry Ringo?"

That was the question. They came down on, "Maybe."

Lora overheard them and laughed. "You girls." Some boys had come over to the house to watch *Ed Sullivan* the night the Beatles were on, and Lora had stayed in the room, but there were three of them, not one, and she noticed with joy and relief mixed that Josie's eyes never left the TV.

— IX —

"SIX ONE SEVEN ONE"

There were no other close calls for Josie in high school, nothing to ruin her life or burn Lora at the stake of public opinion.

Plenty of fun and games, though. The calendar said 1965, then 1966, but at her country school, it was still the fifties. The cutest boy there was a senior named Jimmy Clark, and though Josie had never spoken to him at school, it was fun when he started calling her. In fact, his calls became the high point of her day, those long, interesting, semi-flirtatious talks in the evening. She would sit in the dark in her bedroom, twisting the phone cord, watching the light from the cars that passed now and then in the distance go up the walls, across the ceiling, down again.

It was funny—she'd never really thought much about Jimmy Clark. She'd heard he was dumb—he looked dumb, had a dumb look on his handsome face that had never attracted her. But at night, on the phone, it turned out that he was smart, and cool. He listened to jazz. His favorite film was *Dr. Strangelove*. She hadn't seen it yet, but he said he would go again, would take her. There was a dance coming up at the school—she hadn't planned to go, it was a "sock hop" in the gym, too stupid for words, but she said it would be fun to meet there, and after a beat, he agreed. Reluctantly, she realized when she thought about it afterward.

A friend's father drove them there, but she told her friend that she might not need a ride home. Luckily, she didn't mention Jimmy Clark.

Who was across the gym, yukking it up with a group of boys. She smiled at him, waved, but he didn't wave back. Kind of frowned and looked away.

Strange. She stood by the door, uncertain, confused. Weren't they at least friends? The DJ put on "Cherish," and Jimmy Clark walked over to one of the cheerleaders and asked her to dance.

Put his arms around her waist, both arms. The cheerleader put hers around his neck. Lovey-dovey, to "Cherish," no less, the stupidest song ever. Josie watched for a moment—they were barely dancing. Just standing there, pressed together, dumb looks on both faces.

Did this guy really listen to jazz? On the phone, he'd told her he was reading *Stranger in a Strange Land*. And here he was, mooning to "Cherish" with a cheerleader. It made no sense.

And then she got it. When the dance ended, she went up to him. "You never called me, did you?"

He looked at her as if she'd woken him up from a doze in a haystack, and wrinkled his untroubled brow. "Huh?"

And as they stood there face-to-face, she realized too that whoever it was who had been calling her was somewhere in that gym, watching the scene unfold, and now knew that she knew, and would never call her again.

He was probably one of the skinny guys over in the corner with bad skin, but smart and cool underneath it all. Probably the smartest and coolest guy there that night, but underground with his smartness and coolness, and she had a wild thought to take out an ad in the school paper and tell him she'd rather talk to him than Jimmy Clark any day.

Still, it was also possible that she'd been made a fool of, and maybe he wasn't underground at all. Maybe he was one of the cool guys, one of the seniors, over there with the rest of them, laughing at her. Maybe he'd told his friends— maybe all those senior boys were laughing. Waiting for her to approach poor Jimmy Clark, waiting for the "Huh?" and now laughing their asses off.

She was on her way out to the pay phone, to call Lora to pick her up, when the DJ put on "Shotgun," and a younger boy touched her arm. A sophomore.

She wheeled, furious.

He smiled, almost shyly. "Come on."

They'd been playing the Monkees and "Red Rubber Ball," jitterbug stuff, but now Junior Walker was singing, "*Shotgun!*" or more shouting, and she looked at the younger boy for a second and then shrugged and went out onto the dance floor with him.

"*Shoot 'em 'fore they run, now*"—Bennie Mae Makupson, who was working for them then, loved this song, and she'd taught her and Willie her version of the dance, and Josie took it to the sock hop that night. The hands shooting the gun behind her back. Switching sides. Moving forward, moving back. The younger boy started following her.

"*We're gonna break it down, baby, now,*" she started singing, and then, fool or no fool, she was out there on the dance floor that night. Despite all the faux–Jimmy Clarks of the world, she was dancing to Junior Walker & the All Stars with a younger boy, which was what younger boys were for, she realized—to "*break it down, baby, now,*" as Junior Walker was putting it. To "*load it up, baby,*" high as she wanted it to go. But safe. Untouchable. No younger boy would dare.

"*To dig potatoes*"—she whirled around. One of Bennie's moves. The boy caught on. "*To pick tomatoes*"—what was Junior Walker talking about? Potatoes? Tomatoes? But who cared?

"*Shotgun!!*" Everyone was out there, shouting it now. And though it seemed like just another dance on a Saturday night in middle of nowhere, what was really happening was that the fifties were finally dying in that high school gym that night. It was 1966. They never had another sock hop. No one would have come.

The next year, Josie met some long-haired boys at the local college, who taught her a few simple chords on the guitar, enough for her to sit and play folk songs with them. "*If you miss the train I'm on.*" "*Old Stewball was a racehorse.*"

Fairy tales, but beautiful ones. Serious, sad. "*Bess, the land-lord's daughter.*" "*Come home with me, young Matty Groves.*" Josie was enchanted, in the greenwood again, ready to proclaim her love unto death like Sir Donald's Wife, ready for her black hair to be drenched in her own red blood, like Bess.

But then it was 1967, the Vietnam War heated up, and Josie's little folk group wasn't "*a-marchin' anymore.*" They got kicked out of a local café for shouting, "Hey, hey, LBJ! How many babies did you burn today?" The English teacher gave her an F for an essay against the war. That was okay with Josie, though. Her college applications were in.

"*Don't think twice,*" Dylan was telling her, and she wasn't, at least not about high school anymore. It was the second semester of her senior year. She had applied to some competitive women's colleges, and that was her prayer at night those days.

Let him come had transformed to *Let me get in.*

"Cross your fingers for me!" she said to Bennie, and Bennie said she lived with her fingers crossed, though Josie suspected it wasn't for her, why would it be? She and her family were just the job that Bennie was stuck with, and she tolerated them the best she could. Taught Josie and Willie some dance moves, but more for a laugh during her long winter afternoons ironing. But after dinner, she was up in her room on the third floor, door closed, radio on. No chariots swinging low, no Harriet and Elizabeths for Bennie. If her fingers were crossed, they weren't expecting to find out what for.

Though it turned out they did, one Monday morning that spring. Bennie was professional about her work during the week, and always back on time, come Mondays. Not cheerful or lighthearted like on Fridays, but on time. Resigned to another week of them. But this Monday, the hours rolled on with no Bennie, and they started to wonder. She hadn't given them a home number, and their grandmother was just about to call Sim Richardson, to see if he'd heard anything, when a brand-new sky-blue Cadillac pulled into the driveway and stopped at the front walk. Josie and Will went out onto the porch.

J.C., Bennie's boyfriend, got out of the driver's side in a blue striped suit. "What you looking at?" he said to Will.

"Nice car," Will answered.

"Hey," said J.C. He walked around and opened the door for Bennie, who emerged, resplendent in a tight green strapless dress, cut low in the front. Josie and Will stood speechless.

"Cat got your tongue?" said Bennie.

They walked up to the front door, and when Josie's grandmother came out, Bennie told her that she'd hit it with the numbers.

Josie and Will whooped and shouted, and their grandmother ushered Bennie and J.C. into the living room. Bennie perched on the stiff little sofa, and told them she'd been playing their house number every Saturday night since she started work there, and it had finally hit.

"Six one seven one," said J.C., slow and reverent. Their address. But now brushed with magic.

"What you got to say?" Bennie said to Will. He was fifteen, just getting tall. Still skinny though, still a figure of fun, the way adolescent boys can be. With his cracking voice and big feet. Social unease.

"You look beautiful," Josie risked saying to Bennie,

though there were still those hairs sprouting on her chest, despite the green silk. Josie always wondered why Bennie didn't pluck them. Didn't she know that women were supposed to be hairless? Didn't she care?

But Bennie didn't, she guessed. Bennie made her own rules.

Now she gave Josie one of her rare smiles. "You're going to get lucky too. I brought the luck back to this house!"

Which would turn out to be true. When the college acceptance letters arrived later in the month, Josie got her yes.

But that day, the luck was all Bennie's. Her grandmother sent Josie to the kitchen for coffee and cake, which Bennie and J.C. ate politely, and then got up to leave. She didn't have to tell them she was quitting. Her sky-blue Cadillac wouldn't even speak to their dusty old Buicks back in the garage.

"Come see us," they called after her as she was walking back to the car, though she never did. Will saw her once, a year or so later, when he was waiting at a bus stop. A car slowed down, and he heard someone call out, "Willie Brier!" and it was Bennie, in her old teasing way.

"Bennie!" he yelled, and started running toward her, but the car sped off.

"Was it the Cadillac?" Josie asked him.

"No," said Will. The Cadillac was gone by then.

As Bennie was leaving that day, Josie's grandmother had called after her, "You forgot your clothes, Bennie!" What she kept in the battered old bureau on the third floor.

But Bennie just laughed. "Those rags? Give 'em to the poor!"

— X —

SUZIE

It was later that same spring, her last in town it turned out, that Josie got the letter. It was from a lawyer. "Your father," it started. She took a breath and stopped reading for a moment—how long it had been since she'd heard from him? Years, but how many? She was eighteen now, so maybe ten? Nine? The last time was when he took her to the racetrack, with a woman she hadn't seen before. On a date, Josie figured afterward. The whole thing had been awkward and all she really remembered was looking out the porthole of his new car, from the tiny backseat where she was sitting. A Thunderbird. Turquoise. A color she liked.

And after that? Well, he'd sent her a dress for her twelfth birthday. It wasn't the kind she wore anymore—Lora was taking her to Cleveland by then for nice cotton or wool Lanz dresses, and the one her father sent was a printed pink

131

silk, with a full skirt. Still, it was the right size—"He must have gone to Mrs. Neff at McKelvey's," her grandmother sniffed, and maybe he had, but anyway, she liked it and wore it to her birthday party. And there'd been a pair of white roller skates, the indoor kind, that she'd wanted but that Lora couldn't afford, and a stuffed wool tiger from FAO Schwarz in New York that she'd kept on her bed for a while. But all that was back in the mists of time, so it came as a surprise, really out of the blue, when she got a letter from a lawyer requesting a meeting.

He was so proud of her, the lawyer had written, and wanted to pay for her college education. Could she meet him at the law office in the bank building the next week, to make the arrangements?

She and her grandmother went back and forth on it. On the one hand, Lora could pay for it without him—barely, but she could. Josie's college was $3,100 a year, all in, and Lora's earnings at the school were up to $8,500, since she was now chair of the English Department. And since Josie's grandparents paid all the house bills, Lora didn't have any other expenditures. And on top of that, Josie's uncles had offered to guarantee the tuition if there was ever a problem. They were—Josie was—covered.

But how great, her grandmother suggested to Josie, if Lora was freed of that expense. She could buy some new clothes or take a trip. Go to the Greenbrier for a weekend, or New York to see *Barefoot in the Park* with her actor friend from Philadelphia. He'd invited her, and who knew, said her grandmother, what might come of it.

And it wasn't as if he, Josie's father, didn't owe them! He owed them plenty! He'd never paid alimony, never paid off the mortgage, hardly ever paid child support—

And so on. There was no end to what he owed them, once her grandmother got started. Josie wrote back to the lawyer that afternoon. Yes, she would come.

She and a friend were practicing some folk songs the night before the meeting. "What's wrong?" he asked her. "You look worried."

"Nothing," she said.

"Your father?" he asked.

How did he guess? she wondered. They'd never spoken of her father, not once, her father wasn't part of her life. But what was he seeing, to bring up her father like that, out of the thin air?

When he was nothing to her, nothing. Just the other day, she'd been driving way out in the country with some friends, and she saw a house she hadn't seen before. White, with pillars, but not pretentious. Well proportioned. Discreet.

"That's a nice house," she said. "I wonder who lives there."

Her friends had exchanged a glance. "Your father," one of them said.

And she'd laughed, had to laugh—that's how it was. Her

father was good for a laugh. Although, there must have been something on her face, in her eyes, that night, and she hadn't slept well. Had lain awake a long time, watching the occasional lights from the cars that passed. She went and got her old doll Randall and propped her Raggedy Ann by her side. Said her childhood prayers, not that she was asking for anything. Just to say them.

The next morning, she stood a long time, looking through her closet. Past the Mary Quants, the miniskirts, the wild colors, to her old flowered shirtwaist dress, light blue and white. She hadn't worn it for a while, and she wasn't sure exactly why she put it on that day. Lora looked surprised when she came down, but didn't say anything. Neither of them did—*It's nothing*, they agreed, silently, over the toast and grapefruit. They mentioned the weather—there'd been some talk of rain, and should they put the top up on Lora's old convertible? It took two, at least.

"But it won't rain for a while," said Lora, as she stood on the back steps, looking after Josie, who, costumed like a sweet young schoolgirl, walked out to Lora's car, and with a wave, drove off to see her father at the lawyer's office downtown.

Afterward Josie couldn't remember much besides the pigeons on the ledge, and his voice, scratchy, slightly hoarse, that touched her again before she had her guard quite up.

Had they hugged? Had he kissed her? He might have, to show the lawyer—a loving father. She couldn't remember, even right after. Strangely enough, all she could remember was sitting there, eyes fastened on the pigeons, while he went on about how proud of her he was.

"I always wanted to go to Harvard," she was surprised to hear him saying. She'd never heard anything about him going to Harvard. He'd gone to Ohio University, what people from Ohio did in those days. That was considered fine, great, as good as you could get—should get, and it was. But apparently now she was redeeming his lifelong disappointment by stepping up a rung, going further afield. And he would be happy, honored, to pay for that.

She thanked him—must have, and must have walked out relieved. She had done it, faced him, and it had been worth it. She hadn't realized how scared she had been. Funny, she thought again, that the folk-singing boy had seen it on her face the night before. The father-fear.

But the point was, that was that, accomplished, over. Her heart was much lightened as she made her way to the car, parked up the street. Lora would be free, along with their second line of defense, her grandparents, her uncles, of the burden of paying for her college. Her father was a doctor, he had that beautiful house in the country, he could afford it. They'd heard he'd gotten divorced again, but that was his problem, not theirs this time.

Josie needed something—a milkshake, a hamburger, she hadn't eaten much breakfast, and she wondered who might be up for the Moo Shop in the morning. She thought for a moment—Suzie? They hadn't seen each other for a while, but they used to be close, tomboys together in fourth and fifth grade, climbing trees, playing baseball and Capture the Flag with the boys next door. But then Josie had been sent to a different school, out in the country, and Suzie had— what had she done? Kind of stopped going to school at all.

Her father had died suddenly, and Suzie's mother had pivoted from her life as a bridge-playing socialite into running his store. Suzie's father had a candy shop where all the children in town bought their week's candy on Friday afternoons, and the old ladies came in for peanut brittle and chocolate cherries, and Suzie's mother found she liked her days there, more even than bridge and golf, from the early mornings when the deliveries came in, into the evenings, when she found that lighting a cigarette and looking over the books at her late husband's desk trumped sitting alone in front of the TV, watching *My Three Sons*.

Especially since the hired man, who had become, actually, more like a partner, stayed most evenings too, to light her cigarettes "and whatnot," as she put it to Suzie. Although

Suzie hadn't asked—she wasn't looking for answers, but was, rather, making a virtue of necessity with the old car he left parked most days outside their house. Since he'd started driving her mother down to the shop in her father's Cadillac.

He didn't ask any questions either. The first time he noticed that his car was parked heading the other way, he'd raised an eyebrow at her, but hadn't said anything, and Suzie had just smiled. And then, that was that.

It was also the end of school for her. She was seventeen, and Josie had no idea what she did with herself those days, with that car. People were just starting to smoke pot, but Suzie didn't seem to be going down that road. She hadn't let her hair grow long and wild, wasn't walking around in Indian clothes or "seeing the world in a blade of grass." Josie heard she was drinking and playing pool with some of the cool older boys who hung out at the Lamppost. Maybe she was going to the movies. They were showing foreign films at the college. Josie had just seen *Blow-Up*—had Suzie? Did she want to come play tennis with her with no balls?

She drove over to Suzie's house straight from the lawyer's. The hired man's car was there—good, that meant Suzie was still in bed. Josie woke her and said they had to go get burgers and shakes. Suzie didn't ask why. Just tumbled out of bed and threw on some shorts, a shirt. Didn't ask why Josie was dressed in a pressed Villager shirtwaist at eleven in the morning on a nice summer day.

They went in Suzie's hired man's car, which was good, because Josie found that she was still shaking, and right away she spilled some of her milkshake on her dress. Chocolate, on the light blue flowers.

"God," she said.

Suzie looked at her with her cool green eyes. "It's okay," she said.

Suzie wasn't bothering with college, although she was the one who'd already been to Princeton, to a dance with a boy she'd met on a visit to some cousins in Chicago.

"Maybe we'll meet up there," Josie said now to Suzie. Trying to imagine a dance at Princeton. Which, to be honest, was why she was going to college.

But Suzie hadn't needed college for that, nor would she be meeting up with Josie at Princeton or anywhere else, it turned out. She didn't mention it that day, but she was about to get married. Josie was shocked when she heard the news later that summer, but understood—not why Suzie had done it, but why she hadn't wanted to talk about it. The guy was older, but with a lot of money.

Enough? Josie wondered.

"Plenty," her grandmother said.

Her friends who stayed in town told her that they'd started seeing Suzie around the country club, playing golf with their mothers, or bridge in the afternoon. Josie bumped into her once, during Christmas vacation, a year or two later, but she was no longer Suzie. They hugged, but when Suzie smiled at her, it was from a distance, across a dark lake and down a long fairway where Josie had never been.

She got another letter from the lawyer just before she left for college. Dr. Brier, it explained, would not, in fact, be paying for an expensive, East Coast, Harvard-recompensing women's college after all. He would, however, be happy to contribute the equivalent of tuition at a state university, which came to seventy-eight dollars per term, and which he in good faith, would round up to a hundred.

Her grandmother tore the letter in half and threw it into the wastepaper basket, but their lawyer wrote back, "Send the check." No one was watching the mail, though. At that point, it was close to becoming a joke, one they could almost have a laugh over. They would pay the college bill, just like they'd paid everything else, without him. Ha, ha, even Josie might have laughed—her blue and white dress, her upset stomach. Her trembling hands—all of it a joke.

And him, with his dramatic meeting, his Harvard, he the biggest joke of all—especially the next year, when Lora remarried, someone who was willing and able to pay for Josie's college. If her father came creeping around now, inviting her to his lawyer's office, Josie would regret.

"Exceedingly," as she had learned to write. *So sorry, but*

Ms. Josie Brier is either studying Kierkegaard, marching against the war, or driving to Cambridge in the new convertible her stepfather has bought her. So, all things considered, she finds that she must decline the kind invitation to meet her father at his lawyer's office or anywhere else.

Regrets, too, that she could no longer quite picture his face.

PINK CHAMPAGNE

Martin Brier rolled over in bed, thinking that, all things considered, you might say that he'd landed on his feet. There was a very cute girl beside him, sleeping hard, like the young do, and if it hadn't been that easy at first, what had? The divorce?

By that, he meant the first one, with Lora, which had ended up meaning a divorce with that whole world. Her brothers, their friends, almost everyone they knew. True, a few had stood by him, his old friends and some of the new ones. Doctors who weren't from here. His father, although his big-shot uncle, half uncle, the doctor in New York who'd treated JFK, had sent him a tight-ass letter about his and his art-history wife's "disapproval." "Strongly advising" that he "revisit" it.

As if he could have, by then. As if he, Martin Brier, had

invented divorce. As if it were a capital crime. The biggest deal since Eddie Fisher left Debbie Reynolds for Liz Taylor, and could you blame him? he wanted to ask his uncle. Just for a laugh.

And then, by the second time, as if to prove him right, prove that he'd just been ahead of the game, there was barely a ripple. True, his second wife had no family in town. Although what she did have was a much tougher lawyer than Lora had, hence the alimony payments and child support draining his bank account on a monthly basis, straight from the source.

But money wasn't really the problem this time. He hadn't needed to sneak a mortgage on his ex-wife's house to pay for a new one this time. This time, his third wife had money of her own.

Or would, when she came of age. That was the problem, though not for him, and especially not in bed. The other problem was that her father had been one of his friends, one of the guys who'd stuck by him in the worst of the Lora days. And when the friend found out what had happened, what his so-called good friend was doing with his teenage daughter, it hadn't been great.

He'd even made a scene at Martin's office. Called him a seducer, betrayer, "a snake in the grass! Coming around the house to play golf with me, and all the time, you're slithering after my daughter!"

Shouting—Betty had had to come over and shut the door. There were patients in the waiting room.

"She's just a kid! You derailed her whole life! She's supposed to be going back to college—"

He figured it wasn't worth trying to explain to her father that, on the contrary, he'd been the "kid" in bed with her, that she was no kid along those lines. Nor was she ever "going back to college." She'd hated college, hated Columbus, hated the dorm. Found the classes "boring," and the kids "stupid." And since she wasn't joining a sorority or smoking dope and going to protest marches, what was she even doing there?

College "wasn't my thing," as she'd put it to him.

At the club, which was where their paths had crossed. Once Lora had finally remarried and moved to California, he'd found his way back to the country club again, and that was where he'd spotted her, young and tan, in her tennis shorts instead of skirts—why were those mannish shorts so incredibly erotic on a woman? She was thin and hard, in that adolescent way, which she almost was—well, nineteen, but younger-looking, with her pale blond hair cut short and her girl-athlete walk off the tennis court. Her two-handed backhand, fast and tight, and the way she bounced the ball, three times, four times before serving, gauging, considering. In a world of her own. The direct opposite of his wife—the second one.

Whom he could no longer stand. Couldn't even call

back what he'd seen in her in the first place, what he'd been thinking. To leave Lora—how had he ever started down that path? He had even, briefly, found himself suffused with regret, driving past the house, Lora's. His too, after all—wasn't he the one who'd picked it out, gone and met the neighbors, brought in Molly Waldhorn?

And for a while then, when his second marriage was on the rocks, he couldn't figure out what he'd been thinking when he'd walked away from Lora, and all that, the kids, the life, although now he knew. To find himself married to a nineteen-year-old tennis star with a tough, young body and short blond hair, who didn't ask him where he'd been, or complain that he wasn't paying attention or didn't love her anymore, like his second wife.

Which was true—he didn't love her, or even like her. He hadn't been sleeping at home for a while now, even before his tennis girl. He couldn't walk one more time into what she called the "family room," and find the curtains closed at two in the afternoon, with daytime TV on. The cans of Tab littering the so-called "game table"—though it hadn't done much good, by the way, since she was starting to get that little bit fat, despite all the diet crap. The tall, thin redhead he'd left Lora for was gone.

Replaced by someone he almost didn't recognize the other day, when he'd found the door locked and had to ring. She'd come to the door and stood there, staring him down, and for a moment he wasn't sure who this gray-streaked, chunk of a woman could be.

"She'll never remarry," was his first thought, "the alimony will go on forever."

She had that shut-in look that went with the darkened room, the daytime TV, all that Tab. At least she wasn't drinking, but what else was she doing? Everyone was doing something these days. Pot, vodka, LSD, what the hell. Even some doctors he knew. You just didn't take it over the top.

They'd stood there for a moment, staring blankly into each other's faces—and then, "Mart," she'd finally said to him. Gently. His nickname. Good. That meant she wasn't going to start in fighting, not right off the bat at least. A few months back, when she'd found out that he'd had a few dates with one of the girls at the hospital, she'd called the office, and started shouting through the phone at the receptionist who wouldn't put her through. So loudly that the patients in the waiting room had looked up, and the girl had had to put her on hold. Permanently.

That day at the house, though, she'd sat down and crossed her long legs, pushed her hair around a bit, and lit a cigarette. Managed to pull down a smile, and then he could see she was still there, through the layers.

"You want to come back, Mart?" she'd said to him, and he'd said yes, though he didn't. What he wanted, though, was to avoid a scene that day, and get out with some of his clothes—so, "Yeah, let's give it another try," he'd said, smiling at her, and they'd hugged when he left, and she hadn't said anything about the clothes under his arm.

But pretty soon after that, she'd gotten the picture and called a lawyer, and that had been the end of it. The only hitch was that she'd tried to get him to take joint custody of the boy, half and half, which his lawyer had to work to get him out of. It had cost him, though.

He'd been tempted then to call Lora, to tell her. A joke that she'd get, that they could share, maybe even laugh at together. The irony, or was it paradox? How Lora would have fought joint custody with everything she and her meddling parents and her line of brothers and lawyers and judges could muster, while this one, this tough Catholic girl without even the bishop behind her this time, had almost managed to push her kid onto him altogether. Part-time, anyway.

And maybe he could say, after that, if he managed to get Lora to laugh with him, that he'd made a big mistake.

But would she laugh? Or even speak to him? He wasn't sure, couldn't quite picture it. It had been . . . how long? Twelve, thirteen years since he'd left. He had a picture of her somewhere, a snapshot with a white border, Lora smiling, sitting on a sofa in the living room, in a black cocktail dress with a cigarette in her hand—looking terrific, though not exactly like Lora, he had to admit. Since she didn't smoke and she rarely wore black, so a sort of dream Lora, and that's how she'd be, still sitting there, still smoking that cigarette, on the day when, as he'd been intending all along, he went back to her.

He'd played it in his mind and seen it, every detail. The day when his car would turn into their driveway and he would get out and walk up to the front door. With a box of long-stemmed roses, which he would hand to Howard, who would open the front door to him, and usher Dr. Brier into his own house.

He wouldn't look around too much—that would make it less his house—but he would be really glad to be there, within his walls, finally, the dark wood, the right shade of blue, "aqua," Molly Waldhorn had called it, on the walls. He wouldn't be ecstatic, he would just be home, it would just be right, and he would smile to Lora, on the sofa with her cigarette in the living room, and she would get gracefully up, and follow him into the den, where he would sit in his tweed chair and have a sip of the drink that Howard had brought, his—what? What did he used to drink?

It didn't matter. Now it would be a scotch on the rocks, what doctors drank, and maybe the children would come in, and Josie would kiss him—but not the Josie in the lawyer's office. That Josie had been cold, remote, a stranger. Far from what he'd been imagining, when he'd hit on the idea of that meeting. He'd thought she would come in as his Josie, only better, taller, grown up, and without that worried look he'd noticed a few times in her eyes, those tough days, when he was leaving.

Tough for him too. All that scrambling, all those logistics, complications—endless, and the more he fought to get free, the more trapped he became, what with bishops and lawyers and a new wife he'd never exactly wanted, having a child he'd never planned on, and then his own children, left standing on the sidewalk, as everyone in town was happy to tell him—Christ Almighty! Did she think he hadn't felt it too?

But he'd been thinking that all that was behind them. Josie was eighteen now, and the world had given her a big yes. She'd been accepted into a fancy college, and was surely ready to leave the past behind. To sweep into a dingy lawyer's office in a sleek summer dress, sleeveless, pastel, with a nice smile to meet his smile, and maybe even a hug for him.

What the hell? Life was beautiful for her now, and for him too, which was why he was thinking that bygones could be bygones, and he could inch his way back into her life now by paying for her college education. Maybe he'd even make a trip or two to Boston, to visit her.

Take her and some of her new fancy friends to dinner at some dark, expensive restaurant. It would be a treat for her, for them all, him too. *My father*, Josie would say to the other girls.

But then into the lawyer's office had walked not the cool and elegant Josie he'd been picturing, but a stuck-up schoolgirl in a flowered dress, with a furrow in her brow. She didn't hug him. She didn't smile. And he hadn't paid for her college education. Why should he? She hadn't even looked at him.

Although it came to him afterward that maybe he should have. That this was his last chance, that otherwise she was slipping out of his life forever.

And looking at it like that, what did it matter what she was wearing? He should have seen that, should have understood what it would have been like for her, standing there alone in her bedroom, with the ballerina wallpaper that he'd picked out for her all those years ago, how hard it must have been for her to decide how to present herself to a father she hadn't seen in—what? Ten years?

Or maybe eight, but still, a long time in her life, and he could see it now—just hadn't seen it then. Now he could see it clearly, her biting her lip, running through her closet—old dress? New dress? Low-neck, high-neck? Young woman or schoolgirl? That was the question.

And she'd chosen schoolgirl—he should have applauded that, appreciated it. Taken it as a tribute, an attempt to get back to where they'd left off, to where he'd last known her, when they were father and daughter, and not strangers in a law office downtown.

But he hadn't grasped that, he'd missed it, his last chance with Josie. The "saddled horse," as his New Orleans aunts used to say, "who passes only once." Only a fool, they used to say, lets it go by.

Yeah, well, story of his life. He'd sat there for a few minutes after she left, feeling empty, lost, like he had missed something important—well, he had. And when the lawyer cleared his throat and asked if he'd brought his checkbook, they could deal with the whole thing right then, the college tuition, Martin said that he'd forgotten. Would bring it by later.

The lawyer, an old friend, had looked at him hard, then closed the folder. "I'd give my eyeteeth to be able to fix things with my daughter with just a check," he said.

The lawyer's daughter was on drugs, had run away, something. Martin was sorry.

"You're lucky," said the lawyer, and Martin said, yes, he was. He looked at his watch.

"Got a patient"—but he didn't.

He wasn't seeing patients till the afternoon, but he went over to his office anyway, to sit in the dark. What the hell was the lawyer talking about, giving his eyeteeth? Not that he would be giving anything beyond a small portion of the ready cash that lay in his account then.

The problem was, though, that the Josie he'd been planning to give it to was a charming, accomplished Josie with a smile redolent of warmth, of forgiveness, a Josie who knew it had been hard for him too, and whose college education he would be delighted to pay for.

But the Josie who walked in was an unsmiling, unfriendly girl he barely recognized, who might take his money for college, but still refuse to have dinner with him in Boston. Which gave him an escape hole, and he took it like a rat, and didn't write the check. Instead of seizing his moment to actually do something for her and see how that went, for a change. See if that might bring her to him, and if it did, what a prize, what a gift. A daughter.

Well, he didn't, but he was sorry, so sorry that afterward, he sometimes found himself claiming that he had, even maligning her in the process. Complaining that he'd paid for her college education and she hadn't thanked him.

He took a breath. One of those things, and Josie wouldn't be there anyway, he decided, when he went back to see Lora. It would be just the two of them, him and Lora sitting and having a drink, with the den door open onto the back patio, on a lovely June evening.

Nobody near us to see us or hear us, no friends or relations— like the old song, exactly. Just him and Lora, like he'd envisioned it when he'd bought the house. No parents, first and foremost—Christ, the way people had dropped in on them. Friends, parents, just when he'd been ready to walk in that door and let the evening wash over him. Did it ever happen?

Even once? A quiet evening, with them just sitting and having a drink, looking out over his patio?

His house, where he'd really been living all along, or at least planning to go back and live again, his real life with his real wife, Lora. Waiting for him, and she had waited, he'd seen it, all those years when he'd driven by the house, late at night, and slowed down so as to confirm just two cars in the garage, way in the back, hers and her parents' old Buick Special. No dangerous sleek black sports car sniffing around, all those years, or a jaunty VW, which might have been worse. Might have signified the kind of guy who'd want a nice house like his to hang his hat in. A real step up for one of those college professor types.

But no dice, all those years, but then—he'd been shocked, almost desperate, to hear that she was getting remarried. His wife had told him—ex-wife now.

"What?" He'd wheeled on her.

"What, what?" she'd said, laughing in her new way. Harsh, aggressive, Tab in hand. "You're one to talk."

And she was right, but still—Lora, marrying that guy? He knew him, or knew who he was. He wasn't tall or good-looking, was from the other side of town, hadn't even gone to their high school. Hadn't gone to college—didn't he own a junkyard?

"Auto wrecking," his wife corrected him. "He and his brothers are rolling in dough," she added.

Almost triumphantly, and he felt it. An arrow to his heart at the time, he'd admit it, but now he could see that it had worked out for the best after all. If Lora hadn't gotten married and moved to California with the children, he would never have gotten to his tennis girl. He could never have pulled that off under their shocked eyes. Hell, she was Josie's age, or maybe even Will's. It even turned out that Will had gone out with her once or twice.

She'd mentioned it just at the very beginning, when they'd first started talking, before anything had started between them. Said that she was "friends" with his children, had had "a crush" on Will—did that mean kissed him? More? And that her older brother had taken out Josie—did that mean kissed her?

He hadn't asked further. Any talk of his children made him uneasy, for all the reasons, including the fact that everyone else in town seemed to know more about them than he did.

Did you hear, people would say, *about Josie getting into college? About Timmy winning that big race over in Ravenna? That Will and David Turner walked into the country club with shaved heads?*

And, *Yes,* he'd say, he was their father, of course he'd heard, but he hadn't. He was always the last one to hear.

But with the tennis girl, before he'd had a chance to change the subject, she had looked at him and asked if he wanted to have a drink. They were at the club, having finished their games, him golf, her tennis, and he'd laughed and said, "Sure, let me buy you a Shirley Temple," and started toward the Grill Room, but she was the one, he should have mentioned to her father, who had looked at him with a smile and said, "Maybe not here."

He'd taken her to Cherry's, a new place out of town, where they were less likely to be spotted, and after a few drinks, they were no longer talking about his children, and whether or not she or anyone else had or hadn't kissed them. His children were in California now, or at college, or wherever it was that they'd found themselves. As for him, he had his own apartment, and a nineteen-year-old girl who wanted to go home with him.

A girl who wouldn't be nagging at him about this child's play or that child's ball game. A girl who wouldn't be out there shouting about Nixon or Vietnam either. She was that generation, but barely knew who was president or what it had to do with her tennis ranking, which was fine with him. If he came home late, she was sleeping the sleep of a teenager. If he came home early, she was out on the courts or reading the funny papers.

It had been bad at first with her father, had slammed him back, briefly, to that time right after Lora, when this whole world had closed ranks against him. It had taken all these years to worm his way back in, and it scared him to even think about that level of confrontation again. If her father summoned the world against him—his friends, their friends—and cast him back out, into the dark.

But at the end of the day, the guy had backed down. For one thing, he didn't want to see his daughter married to an outcast. Because that was where it had ended up going that day with her father—he had found himself taking cover by insisting that they were engaged, that he was planning to marry her. Which hadn't been remotely true till that moment, but that was how he found himself in the courthouse the next week, with her in a white shirtwaist dress that wouldn't have been out of place on the tennis court, in the days of Althea Gibson, and him in a silk suit that suddenly was making him feel the full-fathom thirty-five years older than his bride that he was.

There hadn't been anything afterward, no reception, not even a glass of champagne. Her mother had shown up in dark glasses, but none of her siblings had come—fine with him, better. All he'd ever really wanted to do with her anyway was take her to bed, though what he wanted to do more than that right then was to run out the door. Even before the "I do," he was replaying the sorry steps, how he'd been trapped into this absurdity. He even thought for one wild moment of Bishop Maguire. Could he be trotted out again, for a successful annulment this time? If the marriage was "unconsummated," which—there being no children. This one was on the pill before he met her—he could plausibly claim.

Or was that a bridge too far for the bishop? And more to the point, was Bishop Maguire even still alive? Not that it mattered, since there wasn't going to be any annulment. He would go back to the apartment with her and take refuge in what they did together. Which was probably worth getting married for, if it had to be.

His third marriage—"Third time's the charm, right?" he'd said to her with a smile as they walked to his car, but she'd looked blank and he wasn't sure she got it, that she'd heard that saying before. That happened with them. The other day he'd said something about "bats in the belfry," and she'd asked him what a belfry was.

"Nothing," he'd said, because it was, these days. Nothing. Now he smiled at her. Here he was. Again.

"We'll get our own champagne," he said. He couldn't find a place to park, and sent her into the state store to buy it—"Something French," he told her, but she came out empty-handed.

"You have to be twenty-one," she said. Of course. He'd forgotten.

He double-parked and went in himself. When he asked for champagne, the guy laughed and raised an eyebrow.

"Contributing to the delinquency of a minor," he said, and pulled a bottle of New York State off the shelf.

"Nothing French?"

"Hey, it's pink," he said. "Best we got."

And it turned out to be not bad, in bed, on ice.

"I've had worse," said Dr. Brier, and his new wife just smiled, because she hadn't. It was her first champagne.

— XII —

GOLF

A scandal like her ex-husband's recent marriage to a teenager has legs and will travel. Lora got the news, but her new husband made a joke, and she had to laugh. They had settled in Beverly Hills and Palm Springs, both filled to the brim with divorces and family scandals. Martin Brier was par for the course out there.

And in New York too, where Josie was living by then. She'd graduated from college with a degree in political science.

"What are you going to do with that?" asked her saintly stepfather, who'd paid for it.

"Revolution," she'd told him with a smile. She was living with a boy she'd met in college and working at a start-up magazine that was putting music and politics together, with the express purpose of changing the world. She'd gotten blank stares from the editorial staff—the art director was seventeen and the publisher a Texan who ended up stealing the Xerox machine—when she pointed out that Shelley's statement about poets being the "unacknowledged legislators of the world" was true about musicians like Dylan and John and Yoko. So when the magazine made that clear, they'd be able to end the war and move on to the Greening of America, for starters.

It was 1973. Josie didn't mention her father's latest escapade to her boyfriend. It wasn't that she was hiding anything, just that he wasn't on her mind, and they had other things to talk about. He had his own parent troubles, for that matter, more active ones. Hers were dormant, as far as she was concerned. Like an old volcano, that you think is spent.

About a year later, though, when her grandfather died, she went back to Ohio for the funeral and found herself floating to her brothers the idea of a meeting with their father. This death in the family, the first one, had awakened her to the possibility—no, the certainty—that he too, their father, would eventually die, and why not have lunch with him first?

"Would that be fun?" she asked Will. Timmy was game, but that was to be expected. As the youngest, he'd been basically unscathed. Josie wasn't sure if he'd ever met their father.

"Do you think we can get his number?" she asked Will. She was about to joke about calling the Medical Dental Bureau, but maybe he wouldn't remember. Or worse, maybe he would, recall the sight of her shivering in her nightgown, seven or eight years old, and calling, calling, sometimes with him beside her, looking anxiously at the phone.

"Should we try his office?" said the grown-up Josie to the grown-up Will. "Maybe he'll take our call." A safe joke. She knew he would now.

But, "Actually, I think I have his number," said Will. He was in med school, in Cleveland. Their father's alma mater. Will said he'd seen him a few times.

This was news to Josie. "How was he?" she asked.

"Driving a Rolls," said Will.

Josie laughed, said she'd heard that too, along with the news that he'd divorced his teenage wife, his third. This whole imbroglio would have been extremely embarrassing to her, to them, had not Martin Brier, with his string of scandals, his cars and his women, his marriages and divorces, been last seen years ago, always diminishing, in their rearview mirror.

He agreed to lunch, somewhere in Cleveland. Years later, when she asked her brothers, no one could remember where. She regretted not having brought an Instamatic. She would give a lot for that snapshot now.

What she did remember, though, was the first moment of meeting. It was in a parking lot, outside the restaurant. The three of them had crawled out of Will's little sports car, in high spirits, proud of themselves, this small adventure they had conjured. Who goes out to meet their father, after half a lifetime? How brave they were, and how untouchable. Definitely untouchable, being the point, Josie was thinking. No need, even, for any armor this time—not even a shirt-waist dress. This man was no threat to them now.

They spotted him standing outside the restaurant, beside his Rolls, chatting up the parking guy.

Josie's first thought was, *He's short!*, but then she realized that it wasn't that he was so short, but more that he wasn't really tall. Father-tall—funny that their meeting seven years ago in the lawyer's office hadn't dispelled that.

But he must have still been sacred to her then. She hadn't been able then to lift her eyes. There, that day, in that drab office, in the actual presence, right there with the arms, the legs, the chest, the voice she had prayed for so many times, she had been overcome, and her gaze had been tethered to the bedraggled pigeons out the lawyer's window.

But this time, here she was, with her brothers, on a sunny day. In the seven years between the lawyer's and here, she had studied philosophy and met interesting people who'd taken her into a future, away from this not-tall man, standing beside his Rolls, in a suit she didn't much like. Brown silk, not the kind her new friends' fathers wore.

She smiled.

He smiled back. She'd once heard her mother compare him to an Italian actor, but who? He had a cigarette in his mouth and a white shirt, open at the collar, silk too. Maybe Massimo Girotti? She'd recently seen *Obsession*.

Timmy was shaking hands with him—"Nice to see you," not *meet you*, so maybe Timmy had met him? Or was too polite to lay it on the line.

There was a resemblance between them—the blue-gray eyes. Something of the build. It had stopped occurring to her that their light eyes, hers and Timmy's, had come from him. Her grandmother had always insisted that they came from her own mother, once a blonde with blue eyes. Their father's almost-blue eyes had been gradually erased.

But there they were, he and Timmy looking—she had to admit it—like father and son. Timmy was smiling, but formally, politely, as he would with any grown-up he was meeting for the first time. Their father was the one who looked delighted, why not? Here were three well-brought-up young persons for him to take to lunch, with a connection he might now safely claim. No begging about to take place in that parking lot. No sobbing, no one clinging to his knees.

They went into the restaurant, and as they were sliding into a banquette, Will asked him something about a microscope.

"Oh yeah." Their father gave his little laugh and mentioned something, and Will stiffened, and said angrily, "What?"

Josie turned to him, puzzled, but before their father could answer, a waitress came by in a little tuxedo costume with a bow tie to ask what they'd like to drink.

"How about champagne cocktails?" said their father. He didn't say, *To celebrate*, which Josie appreciated. So he wasn't nothing.

Timmy glanced at Josie. He was eighteen. The drinking age in Ohio was twenty-one.

But their father smiled at the waitress, and she didn't card them.

"No, thanks," said Will. To the waitress.

"Come on," said Martin, but Will didn't answer, didn't even look at him. Josie was surprised. He'd seemed up for this lunch, though now he glanced at his watch.

Their father didn't seem to notice. When the drinks came, he toasted them all. "Cheers!"

They drank, Will looking the other way, sipping his water.

"So"—their father turned to Timmy—"you're still in school?"

College, Timmy told him, "in Boulder. Colorado."

"Colorado!" Their father loved Colorado. "The mountains, the skiing." He'd love to come visit, take Timmy to Aspen. "You like to ski?"

Timmy did, and so on, small talk. Their father asked Josie about New York. He'd love to come visit there too, it turned out. Asked Josie if she went to plays, if she'd seen *Hair*.

"*When the moon is in the seventh house*," she said, smiling at him, and he smiled back, but she wasn't sure he got it. He mentioned that some of his patients had been to New York to see something.

"On Broadway."

She nodded. Didn't bother to tell him that Broadway was mostly beneath contempt. That even most downtown theater was just too bourgeois for her. Had already decided not to mention that she was working at a counterculture magazine. Didn't realize till afterward that he hadn't asked.

When the waitress came back to take their orders, Will said he wasn't hungry.

"Come on," said their father, "all that med school," but Will refused.

"You can split my club sandwich," said Josie, more out of embarrassment. What was wrong with him? Having a sulk in this booth with a man it was becoming increasingly apparent they barely knew?

Luckily the man didn't seem to notice. He had another drink.

Said he was sorry about their grandfather. Mentioned what an upstanding pillar of the community he'd always been.

"Yes, thanks," answered Josie, as if he, their father, really had been a stranger. As opposed to the very one who'd robbed their grandfather, literally, and broken his daughter's heart along the way. Leaving him, the old man, to pick up the pieces. To move out of his own house and into theirs, his no-good son-in-law's, which was decorated for his son-in-law, not him.

And he'd lived with it, because it was better for the children, and he'd had dinner with them every single night, their grandfather, and was dragged to piano recitals and Little League games, sitting in awkward chairs with men who were fathers, not grandfathers, a generation younger, and thus kept off the wolf that Martin had left lurking around their back door, so yes, true, he had been a pillar of the community. Theirs.

But Josie didn't point this out, just smiled and sipped her second champagne cocktail, while their father went on, telling them a funny story. Finding himself in need of a new house again, he'd bought one up the street from their old one and moved in. They knew the house—stone, prim, with neat flower beds, and a lily pond out back. It had belonged to Miss Sidna Smith, a friend of their grandfather's, who did not, though, like children in her garden. It always took some doing, some scouting, to sneak in and check on the goldfish they regularly dumped in her tiny pond.

Funny that that was where their father lived now—alone, as far as she could tell. Had he called in Molly Waldhorn again? Josie wondered, but of course she must have been long dead. What was he thinking, though, going back there, to that very street, their very block?

She didn't ask him. She could already see, after their first half hour together, that he wouldn't give an answer to anything that would be of interest, not an answer that would be true. So she just listened and laughed politely as he went on about how, when he was ordering cable, he gave their old address by mistake.

"Our address," he said, and Josie and Will exchanged a look, which he didn't, wouldn't, notice. Just as well, she was thinking. What would be the point of it now?

And apparently the cable guy had gone as instructed to their old house, "but the mayor lives there now," said Martin, "did you know?"

They didn't.

"Yeah." He laughed "He sent the guy to the right address. Called me afterward. We had a laugh." He finished his drink. "His sister is a patient of mine."

"The nun," he said, more to Will, but Will still wasn't looking his way.

"Dessert?" asked the waitress.

No, thanks, they all chimed in together. Their uncle had promised them a tennis game that afternoon. But Martin smiled her way.

"What have you got?"

She rattled off a list, including coconut cream pie.

"My favorite," he said, and Josie thought, *Well, at least now I know my own father's favorite dessert.*

The lunch had been fun, in its way—or more, a success. They'd done it, seen him and kept it light. Proved themselves cool, Martin Brier's children, grown up. No hint of unreturned phone calls and broken dates. No fevers or bed-wettings, no crying or pleading in vain.

The thing for the three of them now was the future, and this man had no place in theirs. All that agony around him seemed to be sublimating into a collection of funny stories.

Like the cable guy—ha, ha. Although what Josie was wondering as they walked out was why Lora had fallen for him. True, she was eighteen at the time, but it wasn't as if he were that attractive. Not Josie's type, anyway, with his brown Rolls and his brown silk suit—to match? Was it possible?

Anyway, not her cup of tea, this father of hers. As they were walking out, she had the feeling of a victory lap for her and her brothers. *Veni, vidi, vici,* from ninth grade Latin flashed through her mind. They had come, they had seen him, and they had conquered. Sat down and had lunch like the interesting people they'd grown to be—more interesting than their father. He was a very small-town guy.

He got into his Rolls—"Anyone want a ride?" he asked. Clinging to their pant legs this time.

"Come on," he said, to Timmy, "I'll let you drive." Clearly not wanting to say goodbye. He the one begging.

Call the Medical Dental Bureau, she was tempted to say. A joke, but would he get it?

Anyway, she was preempted by Will cutting in, "No." Definitive. Closed the conversation. Not *No, thanks,* even. Just no.

Josie smiled back at her father, gave a little shrug. *Sorry, but, c'est la vie*. Not even *c'est la guerre* anymore. More a game. Easy.

"'Bye, thanks for lunch, so nice to see you," and a quick kiss on the cheek, as she crammed with Timmy into Will's car.

"Hey, give me a call next week," Martin called to Will.

Who didn't answer, just peeled out of the parking lot.

Josie turned to Will. "Whew." She laughed. No answer. Then, "You weren't very nice to him."

"Whatever," said Will, and she didn't pursue it, figuring

that it wasn't as if it were incomprehensible, his disdain for this man, though afterward he told her what had happened, both the long and the short of it.

The short was that as they were walking in to lunch, Will had asked their father whether he'd returned the microscope that Will had borrowed from his cousin. Apparently you need a microscope in first year med school, they're expensive, and the cousin, a doctor in Athens, Ohio, had loaned his to Will, with some emotion and the caveat that Will take good care of it, as he had fond hopes that his own small son would use this very microscope someday.

Will took this to heart, took it for what it was, an honor and a trust, and was careful, and when the year was up, and he was about to take it to a friend's mother's gift shop to have it wrapped like precious china and sent back, their father asked him about it and said he was going down to visit the cousin and would take it back himself.

Fine, only he didn't. What he told Will, with his little laugh, just as they were walking into the restaurant, was that one of his nurses had a son entering med school who also had need of a microscope, so he'd asked his cousin if Will could have another year, and lobbed the sacred trust off to the nurse's son.

So. Of course. They'd been sitting there, smiling all around, meeting head-on, face-to-face, their father. Besting him, even, Josie had been thinking. Leaving him in the dust, with their tales of college and New York and their lives well beyond his, and Josie was even toning it down, feeling a bit sorry, and all the while he had already dealt a body blow to his first begotten son, stealthily, before they'd got in the door. With his little laugh.

His, "Yeah, I wanted to help out the kid."

Who could argue with that? The big man, the good doctor, helping out a kid. No wonder everyone loved him, married him, covered for him with his wives and girlfriends, and if this unknown kid dropped the microscope out the window or crashed it on his motorcycle or passed it lightly on to the next random nurse's son, it would still be nothing to their father. And when the cousin placed the blame on Will, thought him careless, irresponsible, an abuser of trust—still nothing.

Maybe he would give his little laugh to the cousin who'd loaned it. Might even offer to replace what couldn't be replaced. Something that actually meant something to someone, though nothing to him.

"Damn," she said to Will.

"I can't believe I trusted him to return it."

"I know," said Josie, and tried to think of something to say, something that would help, but what was there? Suggest that Will call the cousin and rat out their father? What can you do with a man like that except stay away from him? Root out any feeling you might have in your heart, burn it, stomp on it, drive a stake through its heart, and then take it way out into the Empty Quarter and let the quicksand suck it down into the most complete oblivion known on earth.

It was late that night that Will told her the rest of the story. It turned out that that lunch—the microscope—was just the closing chapter to what had felt to Will, for a brief moment, like a rapprochement with their father. Or more than that, Josie realized—a chance to make it go away. The pain that had been there before Will could name it, his deprivation, his fatherlessness.

It started when their father heard that Will had been deferred at the highly competitive medical school where he himself had gone, and decided to put forth some effort to get him in. He made some calls, wrote some letters—"My son." Which was how Will moved back to Ohio to enroll, as Martin Brier's son.

Their father started driving up to Cleveland, and taking Will to dinner at a nice old restaurant near the medical school, where he too, he claimed, had sat as a student.

Had he? wondered Josie. With Lora sitting across from him, dark hair shining, smiling, happy, slightly pregnant by then, in those ugly maternity clothes? Or was it some random student nurse, scrubbed and pert, out on a date with a catch, an "unmarried med student," or alternating, both?

None of that figured into the stories that their father was spinning for Will, first about his own days as a student and then as a doctor, and it would have been there, in those sto-ries, that Will would have fallen for him. A man who was as passionate about medicine as Will was, a man who like Will felt that he had been born to be a doctor, a man with whom Will would have had much in common in that way even if there'd been no other connection. But the fact that what they shared had come through their bloodlines, that something from this man had destined him, Will, to be sit-ting there that day, a med student himself, felt, for a while, almost like an answer to an old prayer. Old enough that it wasn't life or death, but still an answer. An unexpected gift.

Their father must have felt it too, or felt something, a new kind of excitement, maybe a better kind, more sub-stantial possibly than the brief bursts of bright pleasure that rocketed across his sky with each new girl, as he still thought them, and then fizzled out. Like that, and was that his fault? he once asked Will. Was he supposed to stand fixed and gazing into what had become nothing, the void? But here he had a son, just the kind he liked, a colleague-son, smart, funny, good-looking—was there some resem-blance? Will told Josie he would occasionally ask people if they looked alike.

Doctors he knew at the med school, waitresses in the restaurant they both liked. He was finding weekly excuses that fall and winter to drive up and take Will to dinner. They talked shop, both with passion. Their father hung on

Will's accounts of his classes, and Will on his father's stories about patients and his work at the hospital. This level of simple commonality felt like high luxury to them both. Their voices shared a characteristic hoarseness; they were the same height, even wore the same size shoes.

Which Will discovered when spring came and their father invited him to come down to play golf.

"At the club," said their father.

At this, Josie looked up—their club, Lora's club. Will's heart must have skipped a beat at this, she figured. Their father had lost his membership with the divorce, but must have been rehabilitated, and after all, why not? Lora had remarried, and moved to California. Their grandparents had also moved away. So who was left in that small town to see to the old family grudges, or even to blame the current members for letting bygones be bygones?

Except for the three of them, staunch Lora-ites, and that was what Will had to confront. Had to weigh what would be lost if he gave in and was seen in their father's company among old family friends and allies. It would definitely be chalked up as a victory for that side, the other side, enemies till now. Their father and his much smaller coterie of loyalists. Lesser types, down their totem pole, no question.

And if he showed up at the club with their father, did that mean he was in that camp as well? Would he sit at the bar in the Grill Room with men his uncles would never have had a drink with?

And there was also the fact that he had never once in his life either played or thought about playing golf. He'd played football and run track in school, and ridden his bike through the Colorado mountains in college, in an occasional cloud of marijuana to the soundtrack of the Grateful Dead. About as far from golf as you could get.

But there weren't mountains for his kind of bike rides in Ohio, and when their father offered to loan him some clubs and get him lessons, Will told himself that maybe it would make sense here, he could try, anyway—why not?

"Sure, maybe," he said to his father, though the truth was, it had struck a chord. Golf. With his father. What he hadn't had. People's fathers had played golf when he was growing up, everyone's father. After their games, they would come in and pick up their children, to take them to supper or ice cream. Him too, if he was there, among them. And it was always fun, those men were happy, his friends' fathers. They'd all fought in the war and came back to practice law or run small businesses, clothing stores or insurance offices. They went to work in the morning and came home at night. They owned their own houses, and their wives stayed home. They had dinners together at the club all summer. Luaus and Fourth-of-Julys to keep it going. Come winter, they'd take a weekend or two skiing at Seven

Springs. They weren't much good, but the kids were. That meant much to these men.

It started occurring to Will that this life, the one that he knew best, had grown up inside, even if once removed, might be a good one. Might be the best life since the beginning of time.

Will told Josie that he had to fight the feeling that he was a turncoat the first time he walked into the men's locker room with their father. But on the other hand, the golf shoes fit him, and he wore them out of the clubhouse that day, as he followed their father down the windy path, out onto the leafy old golf course.

Josie could see it. Neither she nor Will had ever ventured out beyond the edge of it, all through their own summers growing up in that town, at that club. Even though it had enfolded the pool and the snack shack, where they'd run for their hot dogs and Boston coolers, that beautiful old golf course belonged to the fathers. The tall, stately trees, leafy, green, were impenetrable, off-limits to them. The course was said to be the best in the area, the hardest. She and her brothers would hear their friends' fathers in their golf shorts talking about "breaking eighty." It was one of the mysteries of their young lives.

There were a few mothers too, the sporty ones, in their

dresses with matching little short-sleeved sweaters, on "ladies' days," during the week, when they were permitted onto the sacred premises. There were still a few of those outfits in Lora's closet, after the divorce, though that had marked the end of golf for her. Still, Josie had been consoled by the sight of them there. That her mother had once had her place in that world.

Did that same bell toll softly for Will that summer, she wondered, as he walked through those sacred groves with their father? She imagined him after golf, diving into the freezing pool of their childhood, with the light blue painted concrete gutters that used to border swimming pools in those days, and then having dinner in the Grill Room, walking in with a father by his side, instead of their mother. It must have felt almost like he'd turned back time, had been permitted a redo of the most profound variety. As if a childhood pain so deep it had become orthopedic was being treated, something he was so used to that he no longer even felt it, till it was going away.

Replaced by a warmth that was filling those interior spaces. Moving slowly through his stomach, down his arms and legs, up into his back which no longer troubled him. He sometimes felt a calm smile overtaking his face, unbidden.

He'd been overwrought as a child, often sleepwalked his way to their mother's bed, and had woken even there crying out from bad dreams.

But that was behind him now, and he was looking at a future he'd never anticipated, never dreamed or really wanted, mixed as it was with the past—"except that it was a kind of new past," he told Josie. All that summer, he had the feeling that he was wading into calm, clear waters, "like a northern lake, deep and blue, with that silver light, but warm."

Fatherland, she was thinking. Water that would have been cold somehow magically warm. She'd had that feeling too, way back at the beginning. Cottages at the lake when he still loved them. Mornings when he'd let her in his bed, let her breathe in his chest, his V-neck undershirt. Let her see the way he folded his paper, or struck a match, the way men did it. The time he told her that a marshy pond they'd passed was a "lagoon," where mermaids lived. It was the first time she'd heard the word "lagoon." It still held its power.

Fatherland. That summer, Will and their father decided that they were going to work together. A life was unfolding for Will with a father who liked him, approved of him, wanted him around, instead of pushing him away. Instead of calling for someone to take him upstairs, into the other room, away from him.

Now their father was the one seeking his company, delighted to have this ready-made son with no fevers or colds or tears to wipe. No games to coach, no in-laws or birthdays—in fact, the opposite of in-laws and birthdays and the rest of it. Instead, they could just go out on the golf course and talk about medicine and the weather: Thunder? Lightning? That and the practice they would set up together. The Doctors Brier.

All through that one summer, Will was seeing it. Himself living a version of their father's life—a doctor on staff at St. Hilary's Hospital, with a nice house, maybe even their old house, in this nice town where everyone knew them, with his old friends all around and the club for golf. He had two friends with beautiful sisters. He would marry one of them.

And he'd have a father—he hadn't been able to say that word growing up. But now it would be his. *My father and I want you to get an X-ray; Take a dose of amoxicillin; Meet us for golf at four.*

My father. Josie wondered briefly what Will had called him, but didn't ask. Since the whole thing had come apart by the time she was hearing about it.

Will told her how the scales began slipping from his eyes, starting with little lies, mostly to other people. "I'm at the hospital," he would overhear Martin saying into the wall phone at the clubhouse.

Why? he almost asked him. It wasn't as if he hadn't earned his time off. He still took his office hours seriously, was really dedicated to his patients, so why lie?

But the more time he spent with him, the more lies he witnessed, piling on, adding up. And then he started finding himself on the receiving end of some of those same sorry excuses—though in his case, their father didn't have the guts to confront him. A nurse would make the call—"Your father is at the hospital"—and after one or two, "Yeah, sure's," Will just let it go.

It was November by then anyway. No more golf in the enchanted woods, what with early snowfalls and winds blowing bleak off the lake. Will had taken a surgery rotation, and was starting to wonder about family practice anyway, and to wonder too if he really wanted to move back home. He gathered soon after that their father had a new girlfriend, and then he heard, not from him, that he'd gotten married again.

Their father only told Will about it afterward, when he was in the middle of that divorce. "I was lonely at Christmas," was how he characterized it. Will didn't even know the woman's name.

The microscope was just the tail end of it. Will had pretty much had it with him anyway, especially after a dinner they'd had together with their father's other son, by his second wife. The boy was fourteen, but small and shy and nice, and their father had criticized him, nonstop, in front of Will through the whole dinner. His grades were bad, he couldn't catch a ball, he didn't shake hands right—the kid didn't say much, just kept his eyes on his plate.

Will had tried to parry it with jokes—"My grades are

worse," "I missed a fly ball and lost a game," and so on—but what he'd really wanted to do was to grab the kid and run with him out of the circle of this man's force field. Their mutual father.

"We were lucky," Will told Josie.

Josie hadn't seen it that way before, but Will was right. They were lucky to have escaped him. There were no unpleasant dinners in their lives, no one criticizing them or anyone. Their grandfather poured the water and had his soup every night, but it was Lora who anchored the table. Motherland, it came to her.

By the time of their lunch, Will had dropped his plans for working with their father. He didn't even have to say any-thing, just let the whole thing fade out, like the will-o'-the-wisp it had always been.

He picked up his own life again, where he'd left off, with his own vision. A life much more interesting, much broader than their father's. After medical school, he moved to Cali-fornia and became a distinguished trauma surgeon there. He had a life on the edge of the Santa Monica Mountains, wild and rugged, a landscape that their father wouldn't have understood. He never picked up a golf club again. He took long hikes and mixed perfect martinis. Tossed rattlesnakes out of his house, spoke the truth, and loved his wife and his children.

Fatherland, but his way.

— XIII —

THE MOVIE STAR

It snowed on the tulips when they were back in Ohio, ten years later, for another funeral, their grandmother's this time. Josie was married and had children by then, and was living in South America. She hadn't seen tulips for years, and when she first arrived, her heart leapt at the sight of them, standing red and tall in her aunt's flower beds. *Ohio! Spring! Why does anyone live anywhere else?*

But the next morning, she awakened to snow, and remembered that side of life there. The cruelty, though she knew the snow wouldn't kill the tulips.

But first hopes, yes. First warm breath of springtime decked by the snow, out there cold on the mat. They wore coats to the cemetery, and this time there was no consolation. When their grandfather had died, he'd been old and sick, but with their grandmother, they lost all the life and fun and resilience she'd brought with her from New York when she'd come out to Ohio to marry their grandfather, in the early 1920s. All those funny New York songs that made it down three generations: "Where Did Robinson Crusoe Go with Friday on Saturday Night?" "Pull Your Shades Down, Marianne."

They sang what they could remember that evening as her requiem, and ate the requisite cakes and sandwiches, drank the whiskey, but still there came a moment when they all fell silent, and they were stricken again with what they'd gathered for, the sheer loss. They'd kept it at bay, with the songs and the remembering, but it rolled back over them then, in that moment of silence, and that was when the grown-ups, as Josie still thought of them, shifted in their seats, got to their feet, and with a few hugs, a few tears, drifted off to bed.

The house got quiet, and most of the lights were off. Josie and her brothers, in from different time zones and either too tired to sleep or not tired yet, stepped outside, into the cold spring night, to look up at the stars. There was much that was familiar here—the shapes of the trees, the tall oaks and beeches, the old brick houses, which felt to them, as much as any place, like home. Almost like home. Not quite. Their uncle's house had a round window, for one thing, and the gardens around here were more mani-cured than theirs had been, less free and overgrown, the set-out flower beds betokening what felt to them like an entirely different approach to life—though it simply could have been the twenty increasingly prosperous years that had passed, and the fact that people who used to send their sons out to mow the lawn now had gardeners.

They walked down the driveway and turned onto a darker side street. Here it felt better right away. The houses were quiet, very few lights, no cars on the road. They came to a house that looked empty, completely unlit, slightly disheveled. There was a "For Sale" sign on the uncut lawn. They stood gazing, held in place by the shutters, slightly off-kilter, and the chimneys, familiar unto every brick.

Josie wondered if whoever had built their house could have built this one too, so familiar was it, almost identical. But there must have been countless houses like this one, put up for prosperous burghers in this part of Ohio in the 1920s. Illinois, Indiana, Wisconsin—three-story brick houses with back staircases for the maids, built by the dozens. In no way notable in this neck of the woods, but she'd lived much of her life by now in places—South America, California—where houses like this one had come to seem like a dream. Almost impossible in real life.

Yet here this one stood, their old house's double, pulling focus before her eyes. All the dreamlike vagueness giving way to the actual thing itself, impossibly perfect, the old mottled red brick, the gray slate roof—that perfect gray, just the way it was supposed to be. The house looked deserted, and she and her brothers walked up the pitted drive, up onto the porch, and looked in through the darkened front windows. They knew what they would see, and there it was—to the left, the wood-paneled dining room with a big fireplace. To the right, a living room lined with bookcases.

They walked around to the back. The brown oak leaves from last fall lay deep and moldy on the walk, and it was a little bit slippery. They stopped at the cellar steps, leading down from outside.

She knew those steps. She had fallen down those steps' doubles, scraped her knees. There seemed a chance that if they went down and turned the handle, the cellar door would open, and they could go upstairs and find beds made up in the bedrooms, and she could take the girl's room, in the front of the house, and the boys would have the bunk beds, right beside.

"I wonder how much they want," said Will.

She turned to him. So he was feeling it, too.

"Probably not much," said Timmy.

No doubt. This four- or five-bedroom house with two chimneys probably cost a fifth of what you'd pay for a mildewed shack in Malibu.

They could probably even put together the money to buy it and live here, on and off, just them, no husbands, wives, children. No one who couldn't take full measure of every detail, every inch of the place, inside and out. No one who hadn't sung "Swing Low" with Margaret or danced the Shotgun with Bennie. Hadn't stood on the street in undiluted desperate longing for a man who didn't come, or roasted weenies joyfully out back over a burning pile of leaves with the women who held their lives together. Ridden in their old convertible through streets still streaked with snow, but top down, heat blasting— spring would come!

Yes, that would be the deal. If you didn't know Sim Richardson's dark bald head with the white hair like snow in November, don't bother to apply. If you never laced your skates in the little hut at the top of the hill in the park or watched the chimney of the recluse's house next door turn into an owl on Halloween, or lay in bed with chicken pox, measles, and mumps—

"Let's go," said Timmy. His plane was early, first thing in the morning.

Of course. Planes in the morning, as opposed to crazy mystic schemings in the night. Desperate attempts to strike roots again here, since there had proved thus far to be nowhere else. Nowhere on earth where she lived.

It was on the way back to their uncle's that she noticed the groupings of trees, the beeches and oaks, as they must have stood before the settlers. In stands, the ones that had been left in place when these houses were built. Divided by fences during the day, but the fences dissolved in the night, and the ancient forest took hold once more.

The next day, she called their father. When he answered, she had to suppress an upwelling of joy at the scratchy voice.

He'd heard that her grandmother had died, he said, and was hoping that she might call.

She told him she was here for one more day, and asked if he could come to Cleveland for lunch. It was snowing—lightly, but she hadn't driven in the snow for twenty years.

He hesitated, and then said, sure, great. He suggested they meet at the cosmetic counter at Saks Fifth Avenue, at a nearby mall.

She was taken aback, enough to rush to give him cover, by blurting, "Great," that she had to buy something there anyway. And that part was true—you couldn't get decent lipstick in Brazil.

But still—"The cosmetic counter at Saks?" she said to the cousin who'd offered to drive her there.

Her cousin had laughed. "That's so if you're ugly, he can keep walking."

She laughed—"Exactly!"—but what the hell? Suggesting a cosmetic counter like she was a blind date?

"What if I don't recognize him?" she'd said to Will. The

consensus at the house had been that their father had just suggested Saks as an easy meeting place before taking her to some fancy restaurant. Her uncle was betting on Fire, the new place in Shaker Square, with a sommelier and the best fish in town.

Neither of her brothers had taken the bait for another lunch. But they were right, she was realizing. This had been a bad idea.

"I might not recognize him," she said to Will.

"You'll recognize him. Those eyes."

And she did. He had on a herringbone coat, black and white, an old one, the kind she liked, and yes, "Those eyes." She was nearly forty by then, he was close to seventy, and still handsome, although no longer looking like an Italian movie star. She hadn't brought a winter coat, so had borrowed one from her aunt, a mink. It was Cleveland. Women like her aunt had two.

Not quite the thing for the mall, she was thinking as she walked in through the smudged revolving doors, but fine for swishing back out and into her father's Rolls, on their way to wherever he was taking her.

There were throngs of teenage girls, jostling for space at the makeup counter where some young women in white pharmacy coats were promising something guaranteed to rid them all of "blemishes."

She smiled at her father over their heads, and made her

way to him around the crowd. He smiled at her, kissed her lightly, though enough for her to catch the scent that she loved. Not cologne—something from inside. She realized then that her husband had it too. The same evergreen scent.

Was that possible? They couldn't have been more different otherwise. Her husband was tall, her father was short. Her husband blond, her father dark, and so on, spiritually, genetically, diametric opposites in every way but the one that mattered? Scent?

Was that how it worked? Was this most crucial life decision, determining not just personal happiness but future and permanently entangled genealogy, less a rational, considered choice than a surrender to preconscious, inchoate proclivities?

Maybe, she was thinking, as this stranger who smelled just right to her took her arm and steered her not out the door, but into the throng of hectic, disheveled shoppers, and onto the escalator, up.

Where were they going? He couldn't be taking her to lunch in the mall, could he? But maybe there was a nice restaurant up there? Like the old places in Neiman Marcus and Bergdorf's, where dowagers in hats risked their waistlines for the popovers.

But they stepped off the escalator not into a hushed enclave of white tablecloths but the middle of a food court, where he led the way into an airport-style café, cordoned off from the throngs by nothing more than a twisted rope. They sat down, in what felt like—what was—the din of the whole mall, at a table that badly needed wiping.

"This place has great soups," said her father.

"I love soup," she said, brushing some sticky crumbs off the plastic menu.

A waitress approached. Cute, almost young enough to have peeled off from the crowd at the blemish counter downstairs. "Hi, I'm Chrissy," she said, smiling.

Josie's father smiled back. "Chrissy."

Don't marry her, Josie found herself thinking.

"What are the soups today?" she asked.

The girl looked back toward the open kitchen—at what, though? "Great soups," her father had said, but if there were cauldrons bubbling on a blackened French eight-burner, they must be hidden underground, maybe in the parking garage? Because what seemed to be coming from the small open kitchen were more the beeps of microwaves than the sound of one hand stirring.

Chrissy rattled off a list, too many. The dead giveaway of nothing cooking.

Did her father really like this place? Was this his idea of a good place to have one of the few lunches of his life with his eldest and only daughter?

So, a soup. "Onion soup?" Was there a chance?

From Chrissy, a frown, a puzzled, "I don't think so."

"Broccoli," said Josie.

Her father dodged the soup and ordered a tuna melt.

"My favorite," said Chrissy.

The escalator ran close enough beside them that some transgressive shopper could have leaned in and grabbed the stale little roll on which Josie was nevertheless slathering margarine, in an attempt to make something of the lukewarm Knorr that Chrissy had set before her, bits of broccoli floating in the water. She knew about bad food in Cleveland, knew how it could tempt you into eating twice as much, in a bootless, desperate grasp for satisfaction— like her father's tuna melt, normally an unthinkable concoction, but which now, had he gone to the men's room or followed Chrissy back into the kitchen, she would have snatched off his plate.

She took a breath. She was here, having lunch, with her father, for the second time in her adult life, and there he was, sitting across the table, the man himself, in the flesh. He seemed to be going on about some people who had sent her their regards, names she didn't recognize, though. His friends, she guessed.

She asked about his parents, her grandparents. Her relationship with them had been collateral damage in the divorce. Those were the days of lines drawn, sides chosen, and they had sided with their miscreant son and been edged out of Josie's life.

Painful, but more of a gradual loss that was eventually folded into the more acute one, with them simply becoming part of what had been left behind. But now she was interested. Martin's grandfather had come from Paris in the 1870s, to somewhere in Louisiana. This Frenchman had then eventually done well enough to send his five daughters—including Martin's mother, Josie's grandmother—to a girls' school in New Orleans. Fine, great, the beginning of an American success story, but then how on earth had this well-begun grandmother ended up in Ohio?

Married to her grandfather, no less—and how did he get there? He was born in New Haven, but his mother had died when he was young, and his stepmother had managed, Hansel-and-Gretel-style, to stow this superfluous child in an orphanage, from which he ran away at age twelve, to New York, where he survived as a newsboy selling papers around Grand Central.

At least, that's what Josie had read in his obituary, since no one had ever said a word to her about him, including how on earth he had landed in Ohio. And how had he ever met her grandmother? And how had she married him? She had gone to finishing school, he hadn't gotten beyond third grade—what did they talk about? Did they talk? It was so improbable as to seem impossible—their lives, and then her father's, and now hers. She knew this grandfather had served in the Army in Europe in World War I. Maybe after the war he'd been stationed in Louisiana, and they'd met and married, like Scott and Zelda Fitzgerald. A victorious soldier and a bored southern girl, both young and making a natural part of the wild postwar celebration swirling around them, in which they were happy to be caught up. To take their place as a couple among couples, smiling for the flash-bulbs, kissing in the street.

But afterward? From there to Ohio—it seemed impos-sible. She wanted her father to tell her. Had they loved each other? Were they happy when he was young? She couldn't conjure any memories of the two of them together. All she remembered of that grandfather were the bright red cloth poppies he'd bring by their house on Armistice Day, which she'd pin to her coat and wear to school. With a few extras for the teachers, which the old ladies among them had especially loved.

Years later, she learned that his two half brothers had gone to Yale—no newsboys, they—and become distin-guished doctors in New York. One of them had won awards and treated JFK for adrenal issues. This brother had mar-ried not an obscure girl from Louisiana but an English art historian, whose field of study was "Aspects of the Nursing Virgin in the Quattrocento."

"Is that a joke?" a cousin had asked when Josie mentioned it, but she herself had been fascinated, and was hoping to ask her father about this intriguing relative.

Although she realized now, in this mall restaurant, that it was possible that he'd never heard of the Quattrocento. And that if he had, by chance, been invited to this aunt's Fifth Avenue apartment once for supper, it might not have gone particularly well.

A sense of unreality swept over her then. There was her father, in the flesh, sitting within easy reach, and rather than wanting to put her head on his chest, she was wondering how much longer she would have to sit there. She should have left it at the last lunch, the one with her brothers, which had felt like fun, like lunch with a friendly and charming man, till Will had unveiled him as less a charmer than a trickster you wouldn't want to have lunch with twice.

A point her brothers had taken, but since she hadn't, since she was here, what was left and what she wanted from him was at least some personal history, but it was a no-go. What he wanted to talk about was less their shared relatives than people in town she didn't know. Names she'd never even heard—with no connections, not even the relatives of her old friends. New people, maybe doctors at the hospital. He had recently been elected president of the medical staff at the hospital again, he told her. He'd been pushed out, apparently, for some "minor infraction," but the rank and file had rallied and voted him back in.

So there was that, there had always been that. People who worked with him loved him. Dr. Brier. He repeated his story about the cable guy, about giving him the wrong address. "Our house," he said again.

That gave Josie her second opening to point out that it hadn't been his house since the day he left them with a forged mortgage, but she didn't take it. What could you say to a man like that?

Chrissy came back—"Dessert?"

"What have you got?" he asked her.

"Bread pudding."

Josie was shaking her head no, obviously no. Bread pudding in a dirty little mall restaurant?

But, "My favorite," her father said, smiling at Chrissy. She smiled back.

Josie didn't mention the coconut cream, his "favorite" last time. Maybe that was the point with him, that every dessert was his favorite. Or maybe he did it for the waitresses, or maybe it was simply true, or as close as it got.

Lunch was over at last, and Josie figured that at least she'd get home in time for a walk. It would be good to pack, throw everything together while it was still light. Her plane left in the morning.

"Didn't you have to buy something?" her father asked her.

It was true, she'd mentioned lipstick, in her fluster over the cosmetic counter. But there was no way she could see herself standing at the Chanel outpost with this half stranger, and letting his eyes rest on her lips, as she tried to decide between Vamp and Very Vamp.

But she'd forgotten her dress shoes, and her uncle was taking them to dinner that night. They could dip into Saks, she wore a standard size, she could pick up something fairly inexpensive, and pay quickly and over and out. She was trying to remember what tights she'd put on. But something dark, anyway. Nothing intimate.

She slung the mink coat over her shoulders and walked with her father over to the shoe department. She found a pair of simple, low-heeled black pumps—nothing great, but on the other hand, perfect. Cheap and quick, she could even leave them in the closet here. She had good shoes, cool shoes, at home. She told the salesman size eight.

But her father had wandered over to the designer section and come back with a pair of Ferragamos, black suede. Slim and beautifully shaped. He smiled at the salesman, who smiled back. "Size eight," the guy said, and hustled off into the stacks.

She put them on—they were beautiful, he was right. She walked in front of a mirror.

A small group of girls stopped and looked at her. "Ask her," she heard them whispering.

"Are you a movie star?" one of them asked.

"Very minor," she told them, joking, turning to her

father with a smile, to bring him into the joke, but he was talking to the salesman.

What were those girls seeing, though? she wondered. Some aura of glamour must have settled down around her, there in a mall in Cleveland, in an old mink coat and dark pants and a sweater, with her hair undone, not having slept properly for days. So not at her best, but there, in beautiful, very expensive Ferragamo shoes, something had made her a movie star.

Was it her father? Was that what fathers did in the end? Maybe it was—maybe they didn't talk to you, didn't recount family history, didn't even listen to your stories. Just made you into a movie star.

Her father ended up paying for the shoes—she protested, but not overmuch, for all the reasons. Everything he hadn't paid for, hadn't done. At least he could buy these Ferragamos, which had, after all, been his idea. The shoe salesman bowed them out.

As they were leaving, she realized that he was saying goodbye without offering her a ride. He had assumed, naturally enough, that she had driven, that she had a borrowed car parked in the lot, and she had to ask him if he could drop her back at her uncle's house. When he hesitated, she wondered briefly if he'd somehow made an assignation with the waitress, Chrissy. She hadn't bothered to mention a ride back, since it was so close, really just five minutes out of his way, and it didn't occur to her that it would be a problem.

"I could call someone," she offered, but he said, no, of course not, it would be his pleasure, and they walked out into the chill gray parking lot. She scanned for the Rolls, but he led her through the mud-splattered Chevies and Hondas to an old Toyota, rusted and muddy like the rest of them. When he opened her door, he had to clear some junk off her seat. Papers. Empty Coke cans. A few Clark bar wrappers.

She was so shocked, so taken aback that she blurted out, "Clark bars! My favorite!," her father's kind of lie, she realized as she said it. She hadn't seen a Clark bar in thirty years and had never liked them anyway, not even back in the days when she ate Milky Ways or Sky Bars.

"Have one." He scuffled in the back, looking for a new one. She took it and now had to eat it, as he'd had to eat the coconut cream and bread pudding.

I see, said the blind man, she heard Sim Richardson saying, in the back of her head. She saw it all now: His hesitation about the ride. The cheap mall restaurant, with the "great soups." It all fell into place—he had no money.

Could she run back in with the Ferragamos and return them, credit them back to him somehow? She hadn't noticed how he'd paid. A check? Cash? Charge account?

Could she say she just realized that they hurt her feet? That she no longer liked them? That they were no longer the most beautiful shoes she'd ever had? He had found a couple of cans of Coke on the floor in the back, and offered her one, which she took.

"Cheers," he said to her, smiling, carrying it off, and to his credit offering no explanations. The Rolls wasn't in the shop. He wasn't driving one of the nurses' cars. Someone told her later that his ex-wives—he'd married twice more since the last time she'd seen him—hadn't let him off the hook the way Lora had.

"Cheers," she said back, "cheers," and she smiled too, and it turned out that that was their moment. Over Cokes and Clark bars in a wreck of a car, but something. They didn't talk after that.

They drove up to her uncle's house as clouds were gathering. Another unseasonable storm was moving in. The lights were on inside, and the house looked beautiful, warm and welcoming, more so as snowflakes were starting to float down from the gray sky. That's where she was heading when she closed the door on this gloomy old Toyota, with her discreet gray Saks Fifth Avenue bag in hand, holding the deep red box with the shoes that her father had finally bought her when he could no longer afford them.

She didn't remember afterward how they had said goodbye. Had she hugged him, kissed him on the cheek? Across the junk in the car? Maybe not. A sorrow swept over her as she watched him drive off alone, through the slush, into the gray afternoon. She regretted all the vengeance she'd once wished upon him. That he'd rue the day he'd left them, rue having lost them, since they would be the best of everyone, the three children he'd left behind.

Although what she'd really wanted at the time hadn't been vengeance but for him to come back and love them again. Smile upon them all, her, Lora, Will, and Timmy. Walk in the front door and take them in his arms, into his lap, read to them or tell them stories, whatever it was that fathers did after that. She really couldn't say, didn't quite know. Her memory failed her after that first moment.

But now there would be none of that, nor did any of them want it. They no longer had any place in their lives for this superfluous man whom they barely knew. There seemed to be no congruence of taste or inclination, at least none that proved discoverable in a lunch or two. She had a close friend his age with whom she had much in common. They liked the same books, the same food, the same people. He had told her she was "an intellectual," and given her an identity. Her children had learned to swim in his pool. He knew them, knew their names, liked them.

If the two men could be swapped, then she might have a father.

But as for this one, she was overcome now with pity, and

as his car turned the corner and disappeared from her sight, from her life, forever, she figured, she found herself whispering, "*Vai com deus*," Go with God, as people from the interior in Brazil say, by rote, without attaching any special significance. Just a nice, friendly wish, to her, to anyone.

Vai com deus, she whispered after him, with perfect goodwill even if generic, because what, beyond that, was he to her now anyway?

SHIPWRECK

He drove off, not able to watch, to bear watching, as she walked into her uncle's house. He had to hand it to him, his brother-in-law—he'd really done all right for himself, that pipsqueak. He'd followed the path that he, Martin, had beaten to med school, scurried through all the doors that he had left open for him, and now he was a well-respected ophthalmologist in Cleveland, with a nice big house, one of the six-bedroom deals they had on this tree-lined street in the best part of Shaker Heights. With the knockout of a wife and the three kids, and he'd stayed married.

Which, it came to him as he pulled up in front of the house, turned out to be the trick to having the house with a Mercedes in the driveway, and a Volvo, no doubt, in the garage. You stayed married, and there they were, the big trees, nice lawn, and you could see from the lamps already lit inside that his brother-in-law, former, was probably sitting in his own tweed chair, like the one he himself had walked away from at Lora's. Scotch in hand, in his den. The fire already lit, since there was the smoke coming out the chimney. A gray poodle who would yap at the door when Josie went in. Purebred. The whole nine yards.

The American dream that their European father had gotten rolling for them, working hard, raising them nicely, sending them all to college. Only Lora had been derailed— *mea culpa. Maxima.* Jesus. What a train wreck.

Or shipwreck, as one of his naval buddies had put it, when they were out in the Pacific, steaming toward the Marianas. In 1943, he thought it was, or maybe '44. Anyway, their ship was hit, but didn't sink. Most of the men were okay, but one of his friends who'd gone to Harvard quoted a poet who'd said, "Life is shipwreck."

"Yeah, but we didn't sink," he'd answered.

But the guy said that he wasn't talking about "*a* shipwreck." More life "*as* shipwreck."

At the time he'd thought that that was just Harvard speaking, a whole lot of education, though now he knew.

Lora's brothers hadn't wrecked, though. They'd all sailed straight through the storms, through the shoals, around the rocks, and come out with exactly what America had promised them, promised their father, beckoning him from the depths of the Austro-Hungarian Empire when he was just sixteen: *Come to me, work hard and steadily, and I will give you a home. Protect you. Treat you fairly, you will vote and pay your taxes. Rake your leaves, mow your lawn, keep up the neighborhood. Send your children to kindergarten already prepared by the age of five to sit still enough to progress through. Welcome,* the Lady with the Lamp had whispered to the father.

And here was his son, fifty years later, in the nicest house money could buy in the nicest neighborhood in the state. Paid off, presumably, or if not, with the kind of mortgage that only the rich can get, and pay for, month by month, on time. Early.

And here he was, his double, the man who'd married and then betrayed his sister, the man he'd loved as a brother for a time and then must have hated, here he was, his old friend Martin Brier, driving off alone to an empty house that was on the market. Worried that his thirdhand car might not make it, might break down again on the highway in the snow. He'd seen her, his own daughter, looking around in the parking lot—presumably for the Rolls. Ha, ha, the Rolls. As dead and gone as Julius Caesar. Two wives ago, the kind of wives who hire tough lawyers and get their pound of flesh.

Josie had still thought that's who he was, still hadn't put together why they were having lunch at the mall, that it was the only place her dear father could afford at this particular juncture that wasn't a McDonald's. And hadn't she said to him on the phone that she needed some cosmetics, which was what he'd been prepared to pay for, but then she'd pivoted to shoes, and he was trapped.

But it had still been okay—he was still a rich man in there, in Saks, still driving a Rolls when he insisted she try on the Ferragamos. He was still her rich father when he pulled a battered Saks charge card from his wallet, which was cracked and scruffy though you could still make out the initials stamped in gold inside. True, the salesman had frowned—apparently it was an old card, they'd issued new ones—and disappeared into the back somewhere, and he'd had to hold his breath, till the guy came back out with a smile and the shoes in the gray Saks bag, which meant that the card had, by some miracle, gone through.

How he'd pay for it when the bill came was a problem for another day. Maybe it wouldn't come, maybe he'd have moved by then. Anyway, there it was, it had all worked out and he was walking her out, still smiling, still her rich father, sailing ahead under the assumption that she'd borrowed a car from her uncle and driven herself to the mall. And then she let fall that someone had dropped her there, and that she needed a ride home.

He had actually hated her at that moment, as he stood there, stripped naked in the snow, in the parking lot, in front of this stranger who was his daughter, for whom he'd risked much to buy expensive shoes minutes before.

And now for nothing, as he stood, jaw clenched, opening the door of a broken-down Toyota. He had a thought of grabbing the shoes and taking them back, since what was the point, now that she knew? Now that she'd seen?

Josie, his daughter—the name that had always tolled like a bell for him. "Josie." Josephine, but they'd never called her that. Named after his grandmother, from Louisiana. "Josie"—a name that they would find on his heart if they ever cut him open. If he gave his body to science to pay for a burial.

Josie, the one Josie in the world for him, though he hadn't felt much connection to her today. To him, she could have been just another girl he was meeting at Saks, one more person he didn't really know. And when she asked him about his parents, wanting to hear, he felt he didn't know her well enough to tell her the truth. To explain that of all the topics out there, this was the one he had least interest in addressing, particularly with someone who might catch him in a lie.

Because that was the only fun for him there, if he could lie about them. If his mother could be a southern belle, from New Orleans, from a family rich and cultured before the Civil War, or after—sometimes it went that way. And his father from a rich family in New Haven, which, funnily enough, happened to be true although irrelevant in this case and only worked if the listener had never met him. Because his father, known affectionately in Ohio as "Broadway," had the kind of New York accent—"T'oity-Toid Street"—that cast some doubt on the rich family in New Haven.

Well, it could still make a good story, but needed some serious creativity to come out in a way that didn't leave him the son of a former newsboy whose spoken English belonged less to Yale than to the Bowery.

And then came World War I, when his father had ended up, after surviving Meuse-Argonne, in Houma, Louisiana, where in fact the "New Orleans belle" had grown up and was living in enough desperation to marry a functional illiterate in the hopes of—what?

What could his mother have been expecting? He didn't know, since it was never mentioned. And by the time he was born, whatever there had been between the two of them had dissipated, and all their affection was directed at him, their boy.

Well, maybe he could have told it that way, maybe he should have, at least today at lunch. Because whatever shame attached to being the son of the town taxi driver would have had to be shared between them. Her being the granddaughter.

She had barely known this grandfather, and so had evaded any shame growing up. She probably didn't even know that her grandfather drove around the grandfathers of some of her friends. That he picked up the local bigwigs when they were drunk at night, ferried them home, even drove them to Pittsburgh for assignations, always covering for them with their wives.

He, however, knew and had grown up knowing, and, thinking back on it now, was almost ready to forgive himself for the overblown stories he came up with for strangers. Especially at college, in Athens, Ohio, where his aunt, his mother's sister, had married into the local gentry and lived in a mansion, and why bother to tell his new friends that his own upbringing had had a different backdrop? A rental apartment, up the stairs on a backstreet in a poor part of town.

What would be the point of that? Why break the waves that were starting to roll in so nicely? Though today, maybe he should have taken this one chance to come clean, to let it all go, or at least some of it? The whole superstructure of lies he had carried since then, since he was eighteen. In high school, he couldn't lie, since everyone knew who he was, but on the other hand, he was the one with the cashmere sweaters, bought by his mother somehow, when her own sweaters were cheap and threadbare.

Though what good did they do, those sweaters, when everyone there knew where he lived, who his father was? But in college, no one knew, and then in the Navy, where he became a captain, was promoted, showed bravery—was brave. Felt brave. He was on two different ships that were hit and he hadn't panicked, wasn't even scared, just determined to stay alive with everyone around him. His men. He was the last one into the lifeboat. Twice.

And that could have been his life, those moments under fire when what he did was who he was. And there'd been a chance today, he realized now, alone in the chilly car, to shed all the disguises, and say to that girl sitting there, since she was asking, *Yeah, your grandmother, Nana, was poor, your grandfather was poor, we never had any money growing up, we lived in apartments when everyone else I knew, everyone, lived in houses, but she was beautiful, your grandmother,* he could have said. *Like you.*

And he could have added, *She could bake like no one else in town, she made beautiful fancy cookies for your grandfather, the driver, to give out every Christmas to his clients, holding her breath, praying—we were all praying—for Christmas tips. Big enough to carry us into the spring without worrying about eviction, and is that a crime?* he could have asked his daughter. Since if it was, it would have been hers to carry too.

And who knows what she would have said, because in America, it was sort of a crime, for his struggling father to have two successful brothers—half brothers, who hadn't been sent to orphanages but left to grow up in the big house in New Haven and go to Yale rather than Times Square for their education. Who were famous doctors while his father drove a taxi in a town with no taxis. It was a crime in America, or at least deplorable, for a man like that to be barely, just barely, scraping by, with a beautiful wife who, despite having a very rich sister, still had to wear her fingers to the bone, making cookies every Christmas and praying for tips.

But he was charming, my father! he could have said to his daughter. Because she was his daughter, that glamorous stranger in a mink coat. *Your paternal grandfather was charming, everyone loved him and trusted him, and if he couldn't figure out a way to earn money, it isn't a crime after all! Shouldn't be.* She should be proud of him—maybe she was. Maybe she'd heard stories from her friends, whose fathers or probably grandfathers had all loved "Broadway," as they called him.

Maybe his daughter was fine with having a grandfather who was a character. Maybe she remembered the record he'd once made, singing "Give My Regards to Broadway." Everyone had loved it. Maybe she had too. Maybe she would have told him that, if he'd dared let the subject be broached.

But he hadn't. He was so accustomed to protecting himself from that quarter that he'd run instinctively for cover and started talking mindlessly about people in town she didn't even know, and she'd probably been bored, had been bored, he could see it but couldn't help it. Maybe if she'd asked just one more time. About his mother.

He had about an hour's drive left, which would be hard, because his leg was already giving him real trouble. He didn't know what the hell was going on. That is, he did know—diabetic neuropathy, getting worse. He'd been treating an ulcer on his foot that wasn't "responding" for some time, and now it was moving into his joints. His ankle was killing him, the one on the gas. Nothing he could do about it, though—besides go to the doctor. Which he wasn't about to do, at least not yet.

Relinquish his place as the one standing there, fully dressed, Dr. Brier, the one thing he had left? Strip off his clothes and surrender, lie helpless and unmanned on a table like one of his patients, in one of those demonic open "gowns," just because his leg was starting to rot?

A small thing, compared to his dignity as a doctor—a good doctor and respected as such. He was just voted head of Board of Physicians at the hospital, and why hadn't he told her that? He'd mentioned it, true, but hadn't really explained how much it meant to him, although how could he, when he was slipping and sliding all over the place, trying to evade, trying to keep her away?

But why? To have been born into this or that situation—who cared, really? It was possible that she didn't, or that she might be willing to share in what he'd always felt was his primal disgrace. That was the bigger thing he had forgotten today, when he had the chance to talk to her. For once in his life—he might have come clean or even a little bit clean. Lifted the mask for a few hours, just talked honestly to someone who was connected but no longer wanted anything from him. She wasn't an ex-wife or a future one, not a girlfriend, former girlfriend, would-be girlfriend, not even a child anymore.

She was a grown daughter who had gone to college, lived in New York, lived now in Brazil, and was well married, or so he'd heard, with two children. She if anyone might have conjured enough perspective to forgive him a bit, or at least understand. Maybe even have been interested in his life, his work as a doctor. The real joy he got from his work, his office. The hospital, where everything was true, there were no lies. Where he was the one standing over the table, though he probably wouldn't have mentioned that he was the one who would be calling later in the week to get an appointment. To get someone to look at his leg.

Well, he hadn't told her that or anything, really. He had missed his chance—fine. Not for the first time. He'd let it slip with Will too, that time they almost did it, almost got close. Maybe that just wasn't his thing, as they said— getting close to people. Maybe it wasn't his fault, maybe he'd been born that way. *"Alone I am and alone I'll stay,"* he'd once read a French poet in college. His foreign language requirement. The teacher was an old bag who loved medieval poetry. Jesus.

But, funny how that line had stuck. All these years. He even knew the old French: *Seulete suy et seulete veuil estre.* Maybe he should have taken it to heart, never married.

What had it come to, besides all the endless talk about nothing at lunch today, and he'd watched her face getting less familiar, the more he talked. The less she smiled.

Though they had had a smile. It was toward the end of that terrible lunch in that terrible place—though that wasn't his fault, or rather, would never have been his intention. It was just that he somehow had no more money, couldn't afford to take her somewhere nicer, had almost refused her invitation to lunch, but figured that would have been worse, and maybe it would have been. Who knew? Who could ever know anything?

But toward the end, in the midst of all that talk, once she'd gotten through that mortifying soup—but what could he do? How else could he have played it?

But once she was finished and they'd mercifully whisked it away, she had politely let a moment go by, and then had asked about a seashell that she remembered from his mother's house, a beautiful giant conch. Where she first heard the ocean, she told him, long before she ever saw it.

And he had laughed then, a real laugh, happy, honest, true. Unmasked. That's when she'd smiled at him, a real smile, and he recognized her. His daughter. The one he'd always loved. Josie.

So they'd had that, he'd had that, after all. That one moment.

"The seashell!" he'd said to her. "So funny you remembered that. It's the only thing from her house that I kept."

— XV —

"TIME AND SPACE
DO NOT EXIST"
—AUGUST STRINDBERG

"I'd forgotten how hot," Lora was saying to Josie.

"Ohio in the summer." Josie smiled at her. Ten years had passed since they'd last visited for her grandmother's funeral, but thirty years since they'd left town. Enough to loosen much in the way of ties.

But this morning, overcome with the green, with the scent of the mown grass and the song of the midsummer birds, so different from California where they were both living then, they had decided to "drive back" from Cleveland that morning, "just to look around," Lora had said.

They didn't say "home."

"You won't like what you see," Josie's uncle told them. He'd been back not too long ago, and gone looking for the old house where he and Lora had grown up. He'd driven down the street, couldn't find the house, thought maybe

215

he was on the wrong block, drove back around, and finally realized that the nice old frame house with green shutters was gone. It had been torn down, and nothing built in its place.

"There's just an empty lot there now, between Mr. Wells and the Simpsons."

Mr. Wells and the Simpsons, from a hundred years ago. Mr. Wells had worked at the mills and carried a lunch box. Lora had wished her father worked at the mills and carried a lunch box, instead of driving the first car on their block every morning to work in a suit.

The ice man said hello to the Wells children too, knew them by name, since he still delivered ice for their icebox. But Lora's mother had bought an electric refrigerator, so the ice man didn't know her name.

She reminded her brother of that, and they laughed, but the fact that the house was gone was sobering. "Why would they tear it down for nothing?" Lora wondered. Josie's uncle said he'd heard they were trying to shrink the footprint of the town, so as to economize on "services." Light, water—"Like the Third World," said Josie.

But her uncle said that the new mayor, young, Black, was using the word "sustainable."

"Maybe that's the future," said Josie.

"A Rust Belt future," said her uncle.

The Rust Belt—that's what they were now calling her

grandparents' once-thriving, growing piece of America. Their promised land—solid businesses that grew, healthy children who lived and did ever better, friends and relatives who made life even more of a blessing. The long tables at family dinners, the games of cards and evenings on the porch, the old lady teachers at Lora's school, respected and invited to tea. Coffee, rather, with Midwest pie, not English tea cakes. The milkman, the garbage man, the postman, the grocer given socks at Christmas with two-dollar bills. The hairdressers who knew everyone's secrets, the Chinese place on the other side of town. Chop suey and chow mein.

The heart of the Midwest, their Eden. Josie's uncles had moved to Cleveland, which was still hanging in there, with the kind of manufacturers that were moving to "high tech." Universities and museums, even a symphony. But their city had fallen by the wayside.

"And what the hell was the board of directors of Sheet and Tube doing to shore up the mills when all of a sudden there was cheap steel pouring in from God knows where?" asked her uncle. "Nothing. Blaming the unions while those fat cats were sitting in armchairs, taking their cut, not investing a dime, no upgrading, right up to the day they fired everyone in town."

The real welfare queens, Josie was thinking, as they pulled out of the driveway. They would take the old road, Lora had told her brother, who'd smiled and said that he had too. Josie's aunt noted that the new interstate would cut the drive in half, but didn't put too fine a point on it. She knew the power of the scenic in this family.

"Is the candy store still there, in Chagrin Falls?" asked Lora.

"Exactly!" her brother had said with a laugh.

His wife had offered them her Mercedes for the outing, and Josie and Lora climbed in and set off. They picked up Route 422 on Green Road. Fiddling to turn off the air-conditioning, "But remember how it was set," cautioned Lora. It being her sister-in-law's car.

It was already hot, but they opened the windows, to catch the smell of cut hay, of their childhoods.

They found themselves riding not just through space but time. When they got to Chagrin Falls, it was 1968, when "Republican" could still mean Rockefeller and Planned Parenthood. That had changed, but the women there that morning were still walking around with straw Nantucket handbags, in tortoiseshell headbands and Lily skirts, too short for their leathery legs.

"Fun to see them, though." Lora laughed and said she still had the clipping of Josie at a Rockefeller rally here, in 1968, in a mini "Rocky" dress, greeting Senator Brooke who had flown in to support him, in the hopes of stopping Nixon's re-election.

"If only he had," said Lora.

Yes, true, much might have been different, whole trajectories, lives, the fates of nations. But probably not theirs, Lora's and Josie's. There hadn't been much personal price paid yet for the national disasters—crimes, even—in Southeast Asia.

Anyway, Josie herself had swung from Rockefeller to Eugene McCarthy later that summer and had never gone near the Republican Party again. She'd worked for McGovern after college—"Women for McGovern"—and even had her files rifled in the Watergate building. She still wondered what they'd expected to find there.

The burglars had also hit the Vietnam Vets Against the War next door, whose reaction, on national TV, was, "Hey, we *want* you to know what we've got in our files!"

But the point turned out to be that the Watergate burglars neither knew nor cared what were in any of the files, they were just small-time crooks, and even that was nothing to the fact that they, she, Josie, and the vets, one of whom had lost his legs to a land mine, had to watch in disbelief turning to despair as their fellow Americans elected Nixon in a landslide.

And though Josie shuddered to think how these quaint, throwback Ohio women voted, still she couldn't help being happy to see them that morning. To know that they still existed, like the falls, which she and Lora pulled up to watch, as they always had.

They'd both been to Niagara, even Iguaçu—"nothing to this," they agreed, as they watched the water run down the small mill dam, in no way distinguished from so many others throughout the state. But these were their falls and they found it beautiful here. And the candy store was still standing, with its vanilla fudge and chocolate drops, but, "We'll stop on the way back," they decided.

Lora thought she remembered a back road that would cut through to Four Corners, and they took it and came out at an old clapboard hotel where they'd come a few times when Josie was a small child, to meet some of her father's friends from med school for Sunday lunch.

"Or dinner," as Lora said people used to call it, before they said "brunch."

"You wouldn't remember, you were too young," said Lora, but actually, Josie did.

She remembered the white clapboard, the shutters, even the patterned carpet in the nice old dining room. It's just that she'd come to think that she'd dreamt it, since it had formed part of a recurring, half-dream scenario of her try-ing, in her bedroom at night, to call him back. It was one of the places she had grasped at, a sort of prelapsarian scenario that used to haunt her, the places where she'd once sat with her father.

Him in the flesh, not him in her imagination, him with his solid body, his good smell, his smile, his laugh. The way he would fill a space. The emptiness without him.

And even now, in the noonday light, it seemed like a dream. She half expected it to be gone again when they drove back.

But then she found herself saying, "Chicken à la king?" to her mother.

Lora laughed. "Yes! Horrible! And those biscuits. Careful at the turn!" It was one of those two-lane hairpins.

Josie knew this turn. Once when she was seventeen and speeding on her way to a dance in Cleveland, she'd nearly missed it, but one of her friends in the car had shouted, and she'd swerved and turned, way too fast, and skidded through these very Four Corners, scattering the boys pumping gas and the men playing checkers in front of the general store. She could still see them, checkers flying, shouting after her as she peeled away.

Not that that seemed remotely possible to her now. Could there really have been boys pumping gas and men playing checkers on a warm May afternoon in east Ohio as late as, say, 1966, to be shaken from their country torpor by a foolheaded girl in her mother's convertible, Beach Boys blasting from the radio, crashing through in a screech of brakes, a skid of tires, missing the gas pumps by inches—no, impossible! How could it be anything but a dream?

Who could believe a story like that? And yet, here she was, on the spot, and she laughed, thinking about it, and Lora laughed too, because they were both happy to be in the one place on earth where everything was firsthand, where they didn't have to look through anyone else's eyes.

Granted, it had been wonderful to walk, years ago, enchanted, together, into the Louvre, with everything they'd each learned in school. But here there was no schooling required. School was out here. This was the place they knew like they knew their own names, pre-teachers, pre-books, straight from the cradle. Compounded of everyone and everything—great-aunts, distant cousins, friends, friends' dogs, cardinals, robins, buckeye trees. All that had come to them without introduction or explanation. Just their lives.

But about twenty minutes on, Lora suddenly asked, "Are we on the right road?" Because it didn't look like it anymore. Ten miles past Four Corners, they seemed to have run out of landmarks that they knew.

It didn't look unfamiliar, exactly—they both knew the small grim houses too close to the road, built of that yellow brick that Josie still associated with being carsick. But neither of them recognized these exact streets with their tangles of wires crisscrossing each other, like something she used to see in the outback of Brazil. Electricity, but jerry-rigged.

"Did we miss a turn?" her mother was saying, but then they saw the sign: "Girard." Always a bad place. One of the outskirts, as people used to call them, but a poor one.

"Did we use to go through Girard?" asked Lora.

But neither of them could remember. In their minds, 422 was scenic all the way to town, and led them through the rolling countryside, straight to Gypsy Lane, two blocks from their house.

So what were they doing in Girard? Why hadn't they hit Belmont Avenue, the way they used to? Or, now that she thought about it, maybe Belmont was another route? They must have missed a turn. Josie drove on—not at the brisk seventy of her youth, but an out-of-towner's thirty-five, straining to read the street signs.

Finally, they pulled over at the top of a small hill to try to get their bearings. There in front of them stretched what looked to be an industrial wasteland—empty buildings, broken windows, graffiti. All of it surrounded by rows of barbed wire. There were disused rail lines converging, leading in, half torn up, half covered by dirt and weeds. Auschwitz? *Blade Runner*? Where were they?

But, "My God!" said Lora. "It's the mills!"

Was that possible? They climbed out of the car and stood, looking over the wreckage, under the blazing sun. Neither of them could speak.

Was this really the town steelworks, where ten thousand men used to stream in through the gates every morning? Men they knew, people's fathers, men who supported whole families, mothers-in-law, maiden aunts, on what they earned here. Men who walked to work—there were the little mill houses still standing in the background, up the hill, all in a row. Some sort of union dream, they must have been in the thirties. Empty now. Doors banging in the wind.

Lora and Josie stood silent, in all the silence. A car passed—old, rusty. Burning fuel like they all used to, with that smell of leaded gas. You didn't get that anymore in California. They waved, but the old woman at the wheel, eyes glaring front, didn't wave back. Maybe she didn't see them. Maybe she thought they were tourists, grooving to poverty porn.

The old brick buildings were still standing, still looking solid once you looked beyond the rubble. A few of the loading docks were open. Josie had half a thought to clamber through the barbed wire and have a look inside, but the barbs were all whispering, *Tetanus*, and she could taste it, the rust, in the back of her throat.

They got back into their borrowed Mercedes, both of them hating the association with what could only have been taken as a personal affront here. They should be driving what the old woman was driving, some old junker from the auto wrecking yard Lora's husband had once owned, on the far side of town.

The sun was beating down now, and they closed the windows and cranked up the air-conditioning. No lovely scent of new-mown hay in these parts. Josie backed away and continued down the road. Lora knew her way from here.

She told Josie that they used to make all the spikes for the westward-expanding railroads at this very mill, and in the Campbell works, on the South Side. "American history," she said. "They couldn't have gone west without us. And then in the War—we made everything."

All the mills in town were going then, full-blast, day and night, the sky was pink and blue with the smoke.

"The color of prosperity," Lora's father used to say. And what happened? The unions? Big business? Third World steel? All of it? When Josie moved to Brazil in the early eighties, she'd heard that the steelworkers there were happy to be making eight dollars a day. How could America compete with that?

It couldn't, hence the so-called Rust Belt, stretching through western Pennsylvania, across Ohio, Indiana, Illinois. The former steel towns—Bethlehem, Youngstown, Toledo, Gary, even Detroit and on and on. All of them nice places to live when she was a child.

Now you couldn't drink the water. She'd heard the words "Rust Belt," just hadn't taken their full measure till now.

They saw the clock tower in the distance, beyond the hills—downtown. "The Union National!" cried Lora. They were both excited, hoping to find at least some trace of the rational, civilized, familiar world of prosperous people they'd left there, but when they reached Federal Street, the two grand department stores were boarded up, along with the movie theaters, dime store, fancy women's shops, everything. All shuttered, all empty. There wasn't a soul in sight.

Except for outside what looked to be a sort of pawnshop/ liquor store, at the end of the street where Josie's beloved Record Rendezvous used to stand. There were some derelict types leaning outside in the shade, drinking from paper bags. The last men in town, they could have been.

"Central casting," tried Josie, but Lora was looking really stricken. This street had meant something to her, and to Josie too. They could repopulate it from end to end, in their minds' eyes, knew who would have been standing inside every boarded-up shop, who would have been walking in their doors. Themselves, among others. Their parents, their friends.

"Let's drive by the house," said Josie. She'd heard those few blocks had been declared a "historic" something—district, neighborhood—so there was a chance that it would be okay.

But as they turned to drive up lower Fifth Avenue, they found the bridge was down. Gone, with no signs, no warning, no detour marked, and no way across. No one working to fix it, as if there'd never been a bridge. No one out protesting, even—maybe there was no one left in town who remembered it.

"I guess just go around," said Lora, and Josie did, like everyone else must, these days. But there weren't many cars on the road, for that matter. Maybe that's why they didn't fix the bridge. Maybe this was the mayor's new "sustainable future." You drive around, or if you should find yourself on foot, you half slide, half stumble down one edge of a steep ravine, hop the stepping stones across the creek, and clamber up the other side to get from here to there in this part of the park that the gracefully arched Fifth Avenue Bridge used to span.

The detour now took them past the hospital where they'd both been born—her father's hospital, she didn't mention, didn't have to. They were both thinking the same thing.

The hospital had expanded, and now sprawled for

blocks, with cranes and a few men in hard hats—the growth industry here now.

Josie turned onto one of the backstreets and drove past the houses where their friends used to live. Nice old brick, with three and four bedrooms, living rooms, dining rooms, ample porches, though now with old cars rusting in the weeds out front, and the shutters hanging off their hinges. The elm trees that used to line the streets were gone.

These houses had been lived in by grocers and druggists raising doctors and lawyers, but now—who knew? Underpaid health care aides? The unemployed? The desperate?

Josie turned onto their street, and it seemed all right at first. Their neighbors' houses were intact, though there were none of the striped awnings that used to sweep out from the front porches, and the whole place felt strangely deserted. But then she realized it was because all the windows were closed.

Air-conditioning. Hence no awnings, with front porches no longer in play. All the trees around their old house had been chopped down.

Josie and Lora got out of the car, and stood on the sidewalk, heartsick. A neighbor walking a stately black poodle told them that when the mills closed in '77, they took a third of the jobs in the town with them. Everyone, essentially, was out of work, "overnight," she said, and the only way that people could get any money out of their houses was to burn them down and collect insurance. An industry had sprung up to facilitate this, with a team of professional arsonists who were hooked up with the fire inspectors.

"You would just call them up and set a date. They took payment out of the proceeds," she said.

Her, the neighbor's, family had owned the flagship department store in town, when there was one. Now she lived much of the year in Martha's Vineyard. She'd come back to see her mother and walk her dog. They'd kept the house, she said, because her mother wouldn't leave, and it wasn't worth selling.

They hugged, and Lora and Josie drove off slowly. They had hoped to have lunch in one of the old places—the Colonial House, the VFW—but now knew it wasn't worth even driving by. To see more signs hanging askew, more wreckage through broken windows?

"We can stop somewhere on the way back," said Lora, and Josie just nodded. Hard to think about food right then anyway. They decided to pull in at the cemetery. The florist's next door—former florist—had a weird blue light leaking out from the cracks in the shuttered windows. *Crystal meth?* Josie wondered. Would they be safe, walking around there?

Theirs was the only car in the gravel lot. The privet hedges that used to surround the place had been replaced by six feet of chain-link, but the padlock on the gate was hanging open, and they walked in.

It had gotten hotter, and there was no shade. Didn't it used to be nice here? A regular cemetery, with weeping willows, grass, flowers? Now it was just flat dirt, bumpy, empty, except for the graves themselves. A few high, pretentious obelisks, with their vacant tributes—"Alive in Our Hearts"; "We Live to Love You More Each Day"—but those pertaining to her family were straightforward, carved simply with names and dates. They found Lora's grandmother's grave—an ancient crone in a black dress and hat in the family albums, but according to the dates on her tombstone, only sixty-seven when she'd died.

"Old in those days," said Lora.

Josie's grandparents lay next to her, their eighty-plus years a tribute to the American century, and beside them, the cousin who'd drowned as a baby, her little stone particularly heart-wrenching here among the old folks. Belonging more to the older part of the cemetery, which was dotted with small headstones, from the days when life was a vale of tears and the death of a small child was not an uncommon occurrence.

Though for them, in the middle of the twentieth century, that death had stood out as a signal tragedy. They walked on, slowly, through the graves, the stones, with every name a name they knew, every one. Either the dead themselves, or their grandchildren, nieces, nephews. "Look," they started calling to each other, "Cousin Bertha." "Uncle Sam." "Suzie's father!"

They grew inexplicably lighthearted in the run-down graveyard, stepping as lightly as possible through this dust mixed of everyone they'd known and loved, known and hadn't loved. Friends and schoolmates and kick-the-can kids, paperboys and snowball throwers and swimming pals, doctors, lawyers, and teachers. Friends of their mothers and grandmothers, and enemies as well, the invited and the not-invited. A heavenly feast set for them all that day.

That's what Josie was thinking, anyway, when they came upon his grave.

They knew he had died. Someone had called them—several people had called them. Apparently he'd had the kind of diabetes where they cut off your leg, little by little. One of her friends who still lived in town told her how it had gone—first his toes, then his foot, then his leg.

How was that possible, she'd wondered at the time, in America in the mid-nineties, for that to happen to any-one, let alone a doctor? A working doctor, affiliated with a hospital—she could scarcely believe it.

"Martin Brier," read his gravestone. "December 12, 1920–September 17, 1996." And underneath a little tribute: "A Friend to All."

Josie and her mother stood silent for a moment. Then, "Is it a hate crime if I write 'except us'?" Josie asked.

"Josie!" said Lora.

But then she smiled, and Josie smiled, and then started to laugh, and Lora did too. Laughing despite the melancholy of the day, the fact that home, real home, for them both would always be this rusted corner of northeast Ohio, with its steelworks a ruin and downtown a three-block meth lab. And the fact that Josie's father, Lora's first husband, the one she'd loved with all her heart and soul, lay dead here in front of them with his last lie carved on his tombstone.

"Impossible!" said Lora.

And Josie said, yes, "Everything!"

Everything. Absurd, all of it, everything around them, and yet here they stood, with a Mercedes station wagon parked to the side, waiting to take the two of them back to where life had just as improbably carried them along somehow.

They took the interstate back. They would miss the old landmarks, the candy shop, some nice place to have lunch along the way. But neither of them felt like stopping for lunch anymore, as each mile they drove got leafier, taking them back to the land of prosperity.

Lora mentioned to Josie that her father had called her,

a year or so ago. "I was taken off guard, you can imagine," she said.

"Did you recognize his voice?" Josie asked.

Lora said no, and then, "Well, maybe."

She had, Josie knew.

He was calling, said Lora, because he'd seen her from afar, at a wedding in Cleveland, and she was "still beautiful," he said. She told Josie she wasn't sure if he'd ever told her she was beautiful before.

And then he went on to say, "If I'd stayed with you, we'd have had it all."

Lora had taken that as a victory. But Josie had always hated the expression, hated the whole concept of "having it all," nor did she mention how easy it would have been for him to make that call.

A gift lightly given, costing nothing, not even the price of long distance anymore.

On the other hand, it was probably true. If he had stayed with Lora, with them, he would have "had it all"—all, anyway, that mid-century America had to offer. The wife, the kids, the house, the friends. The place in the community. His work, his club, his golf, and whatever else he wanted on the side. There would have been room for that as well.

As it was, he must have died alone. Despite all his wives, there must have been no one there to call the doctor over his sore leg, possibly no one to close his eyes in the end. No one now to lie beside his grave. When his estate was probated, Josie heard that there'd been nothing left. There might have been a time when she'd have wished him that kind of end, but that was so long ago she could hardly call it back.

She tried to remember the last time she'd even wondered about him, or heard anything. It must have been years ago, when a friend who still lived in town came down to Brazil to visit, and mentioned that she'd seen her father.

"Oh, where?" asked Josie, thinking the golf course. A restaurant.

"The hairdresser," said her friend.

"The hairdresser? What was he doing there?"

The friend laughed. "Getting his hair dyed."

As she turned into the driveway at her uncle's house in Cleveland, she told that story to Lora, and they'd laughed again, and then sat in the car for a few more minutes.

They hadn't mourned, either of them, when they'd heard about his death. The news hadn't even moved the dial on their day. Whatever it was that they were doing, they'd continued doing. If the day was a good one, it stayed good.

But it wasn't as if he hadn't loomed large in their lives, and, whatever he was or wasn't, a "friend to all," a man who dyed his hair, and broke his vows and left his children crying on the sidewalk, he was dead now. And the truth was that he'd taken something of them both with him, even if it was just the satisfaction of playing the game and winning.

Him against us. But they were, both of them, adepts at letting go when it came to this man, moving on. Which they had done, happily—Lora well married, the matriarch among her children's children, Josie and her brothers living interesting lives of their choosing. Their late father hadn't met their spouses or children. He was an ever-receding relic of their own receding past. Over and out.

Josie and Lora sat and lingered a bit in the car in the driveway, both reluctant to quite let the day go, with all that had settled between them. A sense of the life they'd lived together, a sense of having prevailed.

Finally, said Lora, "It must be getting late." They were having dinner that night with the whole family. She wanted to nap and shower, and Josie was hoping for a swim. It was summer.

They smiled at each other, and walked through the garden, into the house.

The end.

Although it wasn't, quite. Summer ended, fall came, and Josie had a dream that suggested a different reckoning, that she didn't mention to Lora. She was a small child again, about six or seven, in an enormous and very grand hall but among strangers, who were celebrating something she didn't understand. Her hair was cut short, and she was standing, frightened, bewildered, pushed up against a rough stone wall, lost and alone.

But then, a set of high gilded doors at the far end of the room opened, and in walked her father, like a god, very tall, in beautiful clothes, decked in gold, the light coming off of him. At once, her terror fell away, and overjoyed, with no hesitation, no thought of hesitation, she ran straight into his arms. She was saved.

But instead of picking her up, rescuing her, he shoved her away, right in the middle of her chest, with such violence that she fell back onto the floor—and awoke in her bed, thousands of miles and half a century away from that child, but still out of breath from the shove, still feeling the pain in the center of her chest.

"Are you all right?" her husband asked her.

And she said yes, fine, but she wasn't. She got out of bed, threw water on her face, went upstairs, and, hands shaking, took a cigarette from the freezer. She sat on the deck and looked out over the treetops—California trees, live oak, eucalyptus, not the maples and elms of her childhood, but she was back there, in that realm, nonetheless.

Dragged back, defenseless, despite a lifetime of mitigation, to that bleak quarter where her father still reigned, in all his power. And she realized that he would always be there. He'd come too early and staked his claim, taken possession of that piece of her soul's territory where she would always be the bereft child running to him, and he would always be the sovereign father, shoving her away.

Fatherland.

O fim

ACKNOWLEDGMENTS

To Starling Lawrence, editor unsurpassed.
Thank you.

To John Perkins, first reader. "Let me count the ways."